METAL CHEST

Metal Chest
by Chris Yee

ISBN 978-1-949218-90-9

Published by To The Moon Publishing
www.nerdchomp.com/

To my father

For showing me classics like Bonanza and The Rifleman

Happy Father's Day, Dad!

LEFT TO PERISH

SILAS PRESSED HIS hand against the weathered surface of his metal chest. The faded paint of the pink heart was barely visible under all of the dirt and rust. The faint hum of his dying battery grew weak as he slid his feet along the wooden floor. With no place to charge, his body would soon shut down.

At five percent, his legs would give out. The weight of his torso would tumble over in a hopeless pile of metal. At three percent, he would lose control of his upper body. His arms would dangle from their sockets like two hanging metal sausages. At one percent, his voice would fade, leaving him silent for the last moments of his life. And once his battery reached zero percent, he would leave the mortal world, forever lost in the vast unknown.

But his battery still had eight percent. After everything he had endured, he refused to die in such a manner. His pace was sluggish, but he continued to walk.

A loud chime sounded from inside his chest. The sensor on his oil gauge. He needed some oil to loosen his rusted joints, but there was none in sight. All he saw were signs of false promise in a world that begged for mercy. The hanging crucifixion of Christ, with chunks of marble missing from its face. The green ivy twisting in and out of the shattered stained-glass windows. The rotting altar that overlooked an empty chamber of pews. It had all been abandoned and left to perish.

Sunlight seeped through the hole-ridden roof and glinted off the surface of a dull metal piece that was covered with dust and debris. It was another chest plate, tucked away near the back pew. The remnants of a body. The victim of a horrible war that had ravaged the world. Silas had come across many bodies, both flesh and metal, but the sight still made him cringe. Crimson blood. Pooling oil. Rotting flesh. Rusting steel. He hated it all. It was something he knew he would never get used to.

He walked through the center aisle toward the glint of light that had captured his attention, touching the framework of each pew as he passed. His heavy feet dragged along the old wooden floor, leaving a trail of scratch marks in his path. When he reached the metal chest plate, he slid into the row and sat at the end of the pew. As he had expected, there was more than just a chest plate. There was an entire body.

He wiped off the dust to uncover the Limbys Technologies logo. The symbol was identical to the one imprinted on the corner of his own chest. He tore off the loose chest plate and tossed it aside, exposing the chip and battery, both tangled in a mess of wires. Hopefully, the battery would still have a charge. He reached into his duffel bag and pulled out a pair of wires. At one end there were small knobs similar to a headphone jack. At the other end were metal clamps. He plugged the knobs into his own chest and clamped the other end to opposite sides of the battery.

The power flowed through his entire body like a fiery surge of adrenaline. He nodded with satisfaction, surviving yet another close call. They were becoming a common occurrence in a world that no longer had rules. Today he was lucky, but eventually, his luck would run dry.

His eyes swept the room one last time. To shorten the charge time, he would enter a low-powered state. He wanted to make sure he was alone before doing so. After a thorough scan, he propped himself up against the back of the pew and powered down.

In this state, his body was frozen, but his senses still functioned. With no control of his head or neck, he fixed his view on the front of the altar. He admired the craftsmanship that had once been there. The detailed patterns and intricate carvings. Outside he heard the chatter of birds, serenading each other with songs.

The calm scene was a welcome change from the events of recent days. In a landscape stained with war and violence, calm was a rare treat. Silas sat in the small pew, tucked in the back of the abandoned church, and enjoyed his moment of peace.

*****

The chirping birds were interrupted by the crass sound of human voices. Silas came out of his low-powered slumber and ducked behind the pews. The voices sounded alarmingly close. He poked his head up to scan the room, but no one was around. The church was just as empty as before. The voices were coming from outside.

He unclamped the wires from the lifeless body and tossed them back in his bag. Securing the strap around his shoulder, he tiptoed to the window and peeked outside. There were four men, one on his knees in a red flannel, and three standing in a triangle around him. The man in front wore a black cowboy hat with the brim pulled over his face and a toothpick poking out from his lips. The other two held automatic rifles, both pointed at the man in the flannel.

The man in the hat hawked a loogie and spit on the ground. "What were you thinking, boy? Do you really think we're that stupid?"

Red Flannel chuckled. "What can I say? I guess the whole cowboy thing threw me off. You know this isn't the Wild West, right?"

"You're in no position for jokes. Give me one good reason why I shouldn't blow your brains out."

"You gotta wait for me to draw my gun first," Red Flannel said with a Western twang, waving finger guns in the air. "Rules of the West, right, partner?"

The man by his side slammed the rifle into his back, sending him face-first into the damp soil. The man yanked him up by the collar and whispered into his ear. "You'll keep your mouth shut if you know what's good for you."

"Sorry, no can do."

The man in the cowboy hat punched him in the nose. Blood flew from his mouth in a steady string of red. His head flung back, and his body wobbled from side to side.

When he regained his balance, he stared at the cowboy hat and chuckled again. "I'm sorry. I just can't take you seriously with that thing on your head. Do you do birthday parties?"

"Let's get this over with," the man in the hat said, signaling to the others.

As Silas leaned closer, his hand slipped off the windowsill. A loud clunk echoed out as his metal body slammed against the wooden floor. Terror raced through his mind as he rolled onto his back and stared up at the half-crumbled ceiling. The men outside had surely heard him. He raised his head and glanced out the window. All four men were staring at him. He dropped back down and huddled into a ball.

"There's someone inside," one of the voices said.

"Well, don't just stand there. Go check it out."

Silas scurried on his hands and knees back toward the pews. The sound of his legs on the floor was unbearably loud, but under the stress of unrelenting panic, the noise was out of his control. The doors of the church creaked open, but he refused to look back.

"Hey, Charlie," a gruff voice said. "It looks like we've got a clunker in here. Give me a hand."

Silas had almost reached the back row when two burly men pulled him up off the ground.

"This one's kind of scrawny," said the one named Charlie, "isn't it, Connor? It looks different than the others."

"What, you've never seen a housie before?"

"Nope. It's kind of adorable how scared it is. Just look at it squirm."

Silas shifted back and forth between their two faces. His trembling knees revealed his dread.

"Don't get attached," Connor said. "It's not a puppy. We can't keep it."

Charlie rolled his eyes. "You're acting like I don't know the procedure. I've done this a hundred times." He pointed to Silas's chest. "One bullet, point blank, right to the chest. Kill the chip, kill the clunker. Easy as pie."

"You got it," Connor said, leaning in to examine Silas's chest plate. "Ha! This one's got a pink heart drawn on its chest."

Charlie bent over to look for himself. "I guess the tin man found what he was looking for."

They dragged Silas down the front steps and plopped him in front of the man with the cowboy hat. He glanced at Silas but kept his focus on Red Flannel.

"You two know each other?" he asked, plucking the toothpick from his lips and flicking it aside.

"Joe, I don't think so—" Connor started to say before Joe cut him off.

"Let them answer."

Silas was frozen. He just stared up at Joe, the one who appeared to be in charge, and said nothing.

Red Flannel looked at Silas. His nose was already starting to puff up from the punch he had taken earlier. "The clunker? Sure, why not? We're best buds, which is bad news for you. I've got a clunker on my side. If you don't let me go, this bad boy will tear your arms right out of your sockets."

Joe took another look at Silas, this time scanning up and down. "You're just an old relic, aren't you? A useless household hunk." His eyes wandered to the bag hanging from Silas's shoulder. "Charlie, grab the bag. See what it's got."

Charlie complied, taking the bag, unzipping the top, and rummaging through. "It looks like a bunch of tools," he said. "Pliers, screwdrivers, wires. That kind of stuff."

"That could come in handy," Connor said, peering over. "Does it have a wrench?"

"Yup," Charlie said, pulling one out and holding it up. "A ton of other stuff too. It's a gold mine."

Joe nodded. "Throw it with the other stuff. It looks like today wasn't a total waste after all."

"Hey," Red Flannel said. "Are you saying my stuff is worthless? It took a lot of work to steal that stuff. Thievery is an art, you know."

Joe ignored him, looking up at the sky. "The sun's almost gone." He turned around and started walking away. "Pack up their stuff and meet me with the others. We've still got a long trip ahead of us."

"What do we do with these two?" Connor asked.

"Kill them. But pack up first. If I see even a drop of blood or oil on the goods, it's your head." His wide stance and large hat formed a perfect silhouette against the bright orange sky as he walked away, whistling "Folsom Prison Blues."

Red Flannel cupped his hands around his mouth. "Into the sunset, cowboy!"

Connor backhanded his cheek. "Shut up. You're really getting on my nerves."

"I can't help it. He just makes it so easy. Someone's got to play the smartass around here, and it isn't going to be this clunker." He turned to Silas and nudged his side. "Am I right, buddy?"

Silas stared at the man with no response, still trapped in a surreal state of fear. After everything he had been through, everything he had survived, he would die next to a man who could not keep his mouth shut. He tried to think of something to say. All he could manage was, "Hello."

Red Flannel dramatically pressed his hands to his chest. "Wow. Truly heartwarming last words. Very inspiring."

Connor hit him again, this time harder. "I told you to shut up."

Rubbing his cheek, which was now puffy and red, he turned to Silas and flashed a wink.

Silas tilted his head. What was wrong with this man? His entire demeanor made no sense. How could he be so casual in a situation like this?

When the two men were finished packing their stuff, Charlie walked over and waved his weapon between the two. "Who dies first?"

Connor rolled his eyes. "You always do this. Does it matter who dies first?"

"Yes, it matters. We should have a protocol for this sort of thing."

"Why?" Connor asked, walking past Silas to stand next to Charlie. "They're both going to end up dead. Why does the order matter?"

"Because it just does. The world's a madhouse. We need to keep some kind of order around here."

"And what if we don't? It's not like this madhouse is going to get any madder if you kill one over the other. Whether the clunker dies first or the idiot dies first, our lives go on exactly the same."

"That's not the point," Charlie said. "It's the principle of the matter. If we want to be civilized, we should have a system in place. Without a system, we're just bumbling Neanderthals."

Red Flannel cleared his throat and tapped a finger to his nonexistent wristwatch. "Could you guys speed things up. I'm on a very tight schedule."

The two men glared at him, nodded in agreement, and spoke in unison. "The idiot dies first."

"Finally," Red Flannel said. "I'm glad you two can agree on something."

"God," Connor said, shaking his head. "This guy just doesn't shut up. Do me a favor and shoot him in the mouth."

Charlie sauntered in front of Red Flannel and pointed his rifle between the man's lips. "It would be my pleasure."

Silas turned away. The idea of watching a man get his tonsils blown out was repulsive. He lowered his head and focused on the blades of grass on the ground. All of them similar but not identical. For some unexpected reason, focusing on their differences brought him comfort.

Charlie's finger moved toward the trigger, and a gratified smile crept onto his face. "Time to shut that mouth for good."

But before he could shoot, a loud chime rang from Silas's chest. Another warning that his oil was low. Silas brought his hands to his chest in an attempt to muffle the sound.

A flustered Charlie spun his head to investigate the noise, his rifle veering away from its target. In this small window of opportunity, Red Flannel leapt from his knees and hit the weapon away. A thunderous crash exploded from the barrel, and a fresh bullet drove into the ground, sending a patch of dirt into the air. He swung a fist into Charlie's chin and snatched the gun from his grip.

Connor raised his aim to shoot, but Red Flannel fired a bullet through his neck. He grabbed his throat and fell like a bag of meat. Silas was still turned away, but the grotesque sound of gargling blood sent shivers through his body.

Red Flannel turned to aim at Charlie, who was lying on his back with his hand to his forehead.

"Who dies first?" Red Flannel said. "Well, let's see. I shot your friend Connor, but it sounds like he's not quite there yet. So, I guess you're the lucky one who gets to die first."

Charlie raised a pleading hand. "Please, no—"

The shot roared out, followed by the dampened thud of his corpse on the soft dirt. A lingering hiss escaped

Connor's throat as the man gasped for his last bits of life. And then there was silence.

Red Flannel strapped the rifle over his shoulder and plucked the other from Connor's body. Next, he wandered to the stacked pile of bags. Sitting on top was Silas's duffel bag. The man peeked inside, examined the tools, and hoisted the bag over his other shoulder.

Silas was still on his knees, too shocked to move or speak. When he saw the man in the red flannel take his bag, he jumped to his feet and began to walk forward. The man spun around and aimed at his chest. Silas froze, raising his hands in an act of surrender.

With an entertained smirk, Red Flannel lowered his gun. "You're okay for a clunker. Thanks for the tools." He turned around and ran off.

Silas watched the man trot away, left alone with two dead bodies. Without his tools, he would soon die as well.

MEMORIES

THE GLOW OF the moonlight washed over the street. Buildings and cars abandoned. An empty husk of what used to be the center of a small suburban town. Twisting tree roots had dug into the ground and ripped apart the blacktop roads and concrete sidewalks. Large chunks of asphalt were missing, and vibrant patches of grass were growing in their place. Sheets of moss and ivy engulfed the crumbling houses, growing in a wild frenzy until there was nothing left to consume. Trees grew wherever they chose. In the middle of an intersection. Over the train tracks. Within the waiting room of a local dentist's office. Amidst a war of metal and flesh, mother nature had taken over.

Silas wandered the empty town, looking for a place to scavenge. His brief charge from the church would only last a day at most. Without his wires, he would not be able to replenish his power, even if a brand-new battery fell from the sky and presented itself on a silver platter. His other tools were important as well.

He skimmed the names of the stores as they passed by. *Cow Head Ice Cream. Gerald's Diamonds. Happy Hardware.* The last one caught his eye. He stopped in front of the hardware store and peered through the shattered window. The shelves looked empty from a distance, but it was worth browsing the aisles for scraps.

A cardboard cutout of a cartoon cowboy stood at the entrance of the store. Underneath were large yellow letters:

Howdy! Welcome to Happy Hardware, Partner!

The man with the cowboy hat popped into mind. The others had called him Joe. A frightening fellow. Although, the man with the red flannel had not seemed intimidated, even after a beating to the face.

Silas walked past the cutout and entered the nearest aisle. Wires were a priority. Any additional tools were a luxury.

He ran his fingers along the empty shelves, observing the price tags as he moved along. How many people had actually paid those prices? During the riots, probably none. He reached the end and turned into the next aisle. It was just as empty as the first. He wasn't surprised. Mobs had raided all of the stores the day the war broke out. They tore them apart in a matter of hours. Some had died. Others had endured near-fatal injuries. All to get a flashlight, or a blanket, or the last jar of pickles. It was Black Friday on steroids.

Another chime came from his chest. His body was begging for oil, but there was none around. In a world of scarcity, oil was at the top of the list. He had not seen a fresh supply in over a month. His rusted joints would have to go a few more days in the dry summer heat. Hopefully, *a few more days* would not turn into another full month.

When he reached the end of the second aisle, he found himself standing in front of a mirror, staring at his own reflection. Old. Weathered. Broken. He raised his hand to rub the faded heart on his chest. It was barely visible anymore under the dirt and rust.

A sign to his right showed the paint section of the store. He followed its lead and found a shelf that was almost completely stocked with pails of paint. Of all the items a person would loot in the middle of a mass riot, paint was probably low on the list. Some of the popular colors were gone, but all shades of pink were still there.

He grabbed the first pail and knelt on the floor. The lid was secure, but with a little force it popped right off. Stray drops of wet pink splattered onto the floor as he tossed the lid aside and gazed into the bright soupy mix. Just the color itself conjured strong emotions. Memories from before the war. Memories of his owner, Desmond, and Desmond's daughter, Paige.

Silas would never forget Paige.

Her innocence was infectious. She had watched the world through hopeful eyes in a way that only a child could. Desmond was a good owner and father, but his childlike whimsy had passed long ago. He was the one who provided a home, but it was Paige who really molded Silas. And it was Paige who had drawn a bright pink heart on his chest.

He stared at the paint a moment longer, and then scooped a hefty dollop onto his finger. A thick drop oozed from his hand and plopped back into the can. He brought his finger up to his chest and carefully retraced the heart.

When he was done, he returned to the mirror to inspect his work. It was far from perfect, but it was better than before. Paint never lasted long. Soon, this new coat would fade as well, but it would never disappear. He would make sure of that.

A rumble of voices passed the front of the store. Silas ducked behind the shelf, poking his head up to see. On the other side of the large display window, there was a group of what humans called clunkers. He never liked the term. Instead, he used simmi, short for simulated intelligence.

The simmies were hauling a large cart of supplies. Weapons, scrap metal, and a modest stack of oil jugs. Behind the oil was a small generator.

Silas crept toward the front window and peered at the walking goliaths. They were military. Much more common than the household models. Much larger, too, clearing Silas by at least a foot. Strapped to their backs were automatic rifles, and on their waists were bulky hand cannons. Their armor was hefty, and their chest plates were twice as thick. Just looking at them made his hands tremble.

The monotone chime of his oil gauge rang, spreading past the window and into the streets. In a panic, he ducked below the windowsill.

"Did you hear that?" one of the voices asked. It was deep and mechanical.

"Yeah," said an almost identical voice. "It sounded like an oil gauge."

"I thought we all disabled that stupid sound."

"It came from over there, in the hardware store."

A medley of footsteps thumped on the ground, growing louder as they approached the store. Silas searched the room for an exit. A weapon. A place to hide. But before he could find anything, a simmi stepped in and spotted Silas.

"Look," he said, pointing with his gigantic arm. "It's just a little guy."

The others followed him in. They all looked similar, with a few distinguishing marks. The last to enter had a single red stripe stretched diagonally across his chest. He pushed the others aside to get a better look himself.

"He's harmless," Red Stripe said. His voice was sharper than the others. "Just a runt. Let's keep moving."

As they shuffled out, Silas jumped to his feet. "Wait. May I have some oil?"

Red Stripe spun around to face him again. "Sorry, little guy. No can do."

"I don't need much. Just a little."

"Look, buddy. I know it looks like we have a lot to spare, but we need every single one of these jugs."

Silas stared at the cart. "For what?"

"For New Valley. We're bringing these back on Riley's orders."

"Riley? Do you mean—"

"That's right. The same Riley who led the charge and freed us from a life of servitude."

"You have so much. Even if you spare just one, I'm sure Riley will be satisfied. Or perhaps I could borrow your generator to charge for a bit."

Red Stripe shook his head. "You're a persistent one, aren't you? Do you see this color?" He pointed to the red stripe. "It means I'm in charge. No one other than Riley tells me what to do, especially not a runt like you."

"He's just a housie," another simmi said. This one had dents in his chest. "He doesn't know any better."

"A housie?" someone else asked, pushing through the crowd. This one had a dirt smudge on his face. War paint, perhaps. "Can I see? I've never seen a housie before." He pushed to the front and looked at Silas. "Ha! He's so little."

"I know," Dented Chest said. "He's almost as small as a human."

Dirt Smudge pointed at Silas's chest, scraping off streaks of pink with his finger. "He's got a little pink heart, and the paint is fresh. Is that what you were doing in there, runt? How adorable."

Silas backed away as they all laughed, bumping into the wall behind him.

"I guess this one's got a soft side," Dented Chest said. "I'm surprised you're still alive. Most housies don't last in the wild. I bet you've never even killed a human."

"Enough," Red Stripe said. "We don't have time for this. We have to keep moving." He waved them out. "Come on, let's go."

They shuffled back into the street, and Silas followed. "Wait, can I come with you to New Valley?"

Red Stripe studied his frail body. "Sorry, runt. We're running late enough as it is. You'd only slow us down." He turned his back to join the others.

Again, Silas tried to follow. "But I can—"

This time, Red Stripe whipped around, shooting an intense glare into Silas's eyes. "I said no. We don't have room for you." He leaned in closer and spoke with purpose. "We don't kill our own kind, not even runts like you. Riley would disapprove. But if you test my patience, I'll rip your legs off. Do you understand?"

Silas slouched to the ground and stared up at the giant beast in silence. Not a word. Not a sound.

Red Stripe nodded. "Good." He turned his back and walked out the door.

Silas watched them march away, reflecting on what they had said. They were probably right. He would never make it to New Valley alive. Not on his own.

Red Flannel

S ILAS LEFT THE hardware store and walked further down the block. The moon was at the peak of its arc, casting a mysterious aura over the street of abandoned vehicles.

The cluttered roads reminded him of the word that people had chosen to describe his kind. Clunker. To him, the term was more fit for describing a car. They were relics of the past. Pieces of junk that were only good for scraps. Their batteries were always dead, but there was a small chance that one of them had the wires he was looking for.

He started to open the hood of a car, but the sight of a red flannel shirt caught his attention. It was hanging from the mirror of an old RV, which was skewed across all three lanes. He approached the shirt as it waved in the breeze. The fabric was damp with sweat, and there were blood stains up near the collar.

He peeked through the glass pane in the door, but a layer of dirt obscured his view. The handle was stuck, locked from the inside. Rumbling snores came from within. He wandered to the front, but a large sheet of plywood blocked the windshield and thick blackout curtains covered the side windows.

He stepped back to look from a distance. The sides were streaked with dry mud, and the tires were slashed to shreds. There were large cracks across the windows, and both headlights were smashed. The RV was certainly no longer recreational.

The moonlight glinted off a piece of metal on the back. It was the rounded handle of a ladder, leading up to the roof. At the center of the roof was a standard emergency exit hatch.

With careful attention, he climbed the ladder. His rubber soles squeaked against the chrome rungs. As he stepped across the top of the vehicle, the metal moaned and creaked. For a brief moment, the snoring stopped as the man inside rolled onto his back. Then, the snoring continued.

Silas reached the emergency hatch and leaned against the frame. The hinge snapped at the weight of his body and slid off the side of the roof. It crashed onto the hard pavement and echoed an empty clang. The man shifted in his seat, turning away from the noise and revealing his face.

It was the same man that Silas had met earlier. He was sprawled shirtless across a cushioned seat with his legs propped on a pile of boxes. His face was bruised from the beating he had taken. On the table to his side were guns he had snagged from Charlie and Connor. Behind him were the bags he had stolen, and Silas's tools were sitting on top.

They were impossible to reach from the roof, but if he lowered himself down, he could grab his tools, unlock the door, and go unnoticed. He sat on the edge of the open hatch, dangling his legs through the hole. Carefully, he placed a hand on either side of the opening and lowered himself down until he was hanging. The metal rim of the hatch creaked and started to bend from his weight. As he hung, he kept an eye on the snoring man.

A silent drop from the ceiling was impossible, but with precise timing, perhaps he could mask the sound with the snores. He waited, dangling from the open hatch, studying the rhythm of the man's breath.

…in…out…in…out…

He bobbed his head with the steady tempo, anticipating the perfect moment to drop.

…in…out…in…out…

A piercing chime rang from his chest. He lost his grip and flailed about, yanking the curtain from the wall and falling to the ground. His heavy body crashed to the floor, shaking the entire RV. The silky curtain sprung in the air and floated down over his head.

The man shot up from his seat, eyelids bursting wide open, and reached for one of his rifles. "Don't come any closer," he yelled, "unless you're looking to die!"

Silas threw the curtain aside and scurried back against the wall, throwing his hands up as a sign of surrender. The moonlight shined through the curtainless window, highlighting his rusty chest.

The man glanced at the pink heart, and then at Silas's face. With a close and careful examination, he lowered his gun and cracked a smile. "You're the clunker from before."

Silas did not respond. Instead, he kept his arms raised, staring back at the man.

"Ah, that's right," the man said. "You're the one who doesn't speak. But if I remember, that's not entirely true." He snapped his fingers and pointed. "Hello…Right? That was your one word of wisdom."

Again, Silas did not say a word.

"Hmm. After everything we've been through, you've gone shy on me. I guess I can't *make* you talk, nor do I really care. I apologize for my indecency." He gestured to his shirtless body. "Mr. Cowboy ruined my flannel when he decided to sock me in the face. I got most of the blood out, but the shirt's still damp as hell. I've got it drying outside. But you don't want to hear about laundry. Where are my manners? The name's Deacon." He stuck out his hand.

Silas glanced at his hand but didn't shake it.

"I don't suppose you're going to tell me why you crashed through the ceiling." He paused for an answer, but Silas only stared back at him. "No? Not a word? Look, as much as I like hearing myself talk, I need some kind of back and forth. Otherwise, I'm just some crazy guy talking to a walking trash can."

Coherent words eluded Silas. All he could manage was an awkward shrug.

Deacon mirrored the gesture with a similar, mocking shrug of his own. "Okay, then. I see you're just going to stand there for the rest of the night, so I'm going to find somewhere else to sleep. Good running into you again…I guess."

He slung the rifle over his shoulder and reached for the duffel bag.

"Wait," Silas said. "That's my bag."

Deacon cracked another smile. "So, you do speak. For a second I thought there might be something wrong with your voice modulator thingy."

Silas pointed to the duffel bag. "I need those tools."

"Of course you do, and so do I. You've got some valuable stuff in here. But the bag isn't yours anymore. Those goons may have stolen it from you, but I plucked it from them, fair and square. Finders keepers."

"But I need that bag if I want to reach New Valley."

"New Valley, huh? I hate to break it to you, but a clunker like you is never going to make it all the way to New Valley. I'm a nice dude, but most people would have killed—"

A bullet shattered the curtainless window and dented the corner of Silas's chest plate. He stumbled back and hit a wall. Another bullet whizzed between them, tearing open one of the cabinets. They dropped to the floor and covered their heads, protecting themselves from the raining debris. Two more bullets ripped through the side of the RV and splintered the wooden counter.

"Hold your fire," said a familiar voice.

Deacon's eyes widened when he heard the subtle Western accent. "The son of a bitch found us."

"Are you sure it was them?" asked the voice outside.

"I think so, Joe. A man and a clunker, right?"

"Yeah, that's them." He cleared his throat and raised his voice. "We know you're in there, but you probably figured that out from the bullets. We also know what you did to Charlie and Connor." He waited for a response and then continued. "They didn't deserve what you did to them, you know. They were good guys, just looking out for our community.

"You see, when someone steals from us, we consider that a crime. When someone walks into our camp and waves a gun in our face, we consider them dangerous. I like to think there's still some civility in this world. Civility comes with rules. If you break those rules, you should be punished. Justice must be served."

Again, he waited for a response. This time, Deacon answered.

"Justice, huh? Where's your badge then, sheriff?"

"Enough with the jokes!" Joe screamed. "If you want to be a smartass, so be it." He turned to his men. "Kill them both."

A barrage of bullets tattered the RV. Deacon rose up with his rifle, firing back with rage in his eyes. He threw the second rifle to Silas. "Here!" he yelled over the roar of gunfire. "Let's kill these sons of bitches."

Silas caught the weapon. Its weight was uncomfortably hefty. He aimed through the window, struggling to keep his arm steady. His finger froze, and then crept away from the trigger.

Between shots, Deacon looked at Silas. "You're a freaking clunker for Christ's sake. You should know how to use that thing."

Silas tried again, this time firing a single shot into the ground twenty feet in front of the RV. The recoil swung the barrel upward, and he fired again into the ceiling. Embarrassed, he lowered the gun and slumped his head.

"Really?" Deacon said. "That's the best you've got?"

A bullet crashed through the half-shattered window, piercing Silas's head and blowing off the entire left side of his face. The incredible force pushed him back against the counter, slamming his head into the cabinet. He raised a hand to the missing half of his face and then ducked below cover.

"Holy crap," Deacon said. "Are you okay, buddy?"

Silas nodded and gave a thumbs-up. "Yes, I'm okay."

"Good. There are way too many out there. I'm bailing." He yanked the rifle from Silas. "There's no point in letting you keep this if you're not going to use it. If you want to be helpful, grab the bag and follow me." He slid the bag across the floor. "Don't look back. Just run for your goddamn life. Do you understand?"

"Yes," Silas said, grabbing the bag and looking at Deacon with his one remaining eye.

Deacon bashed through the front door, grabbed his shirt from the side-view mirror, and sprinted into the foggy night. Silas followed, running away from the sound of gunfire. They weaved through a maze of cars, sliding across hoods and spinning around corners.

The shots from behind quickly stopped, replaced by the distant pitter-patter of feet and an occasional barking order from the men. *Find them! Don't let them get away!* Their voices jostled Silas's nerves, but he tried to focus on Deacon. The man was spry for his age. Silas's unoiled joints and recent loss of depth perception made it hard to keep up. Deacon made an abrupt turn into a local police station. Silas almost slid past the door but caught the edge of the corner and swung through.

Inside, Deacon had vanished. Silas stopped to scan the reception area. There was a short counter with a banner in front. The word *Welcome* was printed in large blue letters. Behind, there were rows of empty wooden desks stacked with files and folders. Lining the sides of the room were abandoned offices. He walked through the aisle at a deliberate pace, turning his head from side to side.

Another chime rang from Silas's chest. As if he had been summoned by the sound, Deacon rolled out from under a desk and pulled Silas down with him.

"Can you shut that damn noise off?" he said, pointing to Silas's chest. "You're going to get us killed."

Silas shook his head and shrugged. "I can go somewhere else if you would like," he said, standing up.

Deacon pulled him back down. "Stay down. It's not going to go off again, is it?"

"No, not for a while."

"Good. Then just shut your mouth and we might just get through this alive."

The front door swung open, and a single pair of boots walked through. Outside, a volley of footsteps scurried past the building to look elsewhere. Silas monitored the steps of the man who had entered. He moved to the side of the room and continued along the perimeter. When he reached the far wall, he stopped, turned inward, and moved toward the center.

Silas and Deacon pressed closer to the floor as the brown leather boots stepped into their sights, stopping right in front of them. Silas peeked out to see a bushy gray mustache and overgrown sideburns. The man's hands were hooked on his belt, which was barely holding his plump belly in place.

"Where the hell did they go?" the man asked, swiveling his head. "This is a goddamn waste of time. We could be on the road right now if Joe didn't have his head up his ass about these two idiots. At this rate, we'll be lucky if we get to New Valley this century."

He scoffed, marched down the aisle, and barged out the front door. They could hear him yelling outside. "I've got nothing in here. Did you find anything?" Another voice that was far too distant to understand replied with a muffled whisper.

When the voices were gone, Deacon slid out from under the desk and ran his fingers through his greasy hair. "That was pretty close, huh?"

Silas's oil gauge chimed again as he rose to his feet.

"If that had gone off a minute earlier, we would both be toast right now," Deacon said, poking his finger at Silas's chest. "What is that thing, anyway? Some sort of clunker doohickey I wouldn't understand?"

Silas shook his head. "My oil supply is empty."

As he said this, his legs collapsed under the weight of his body. Deacon leapt forward to catch him, but the metal chassis was too heavy. Silas fell forward into a kneeling position.

"What the hell just happened?" Deacon asked. "Are you okay? That bullet tore up your face pretty bad."

"It has nothing to do with my face. My battery is low. I expelled a lot of energy running. My legs lose function when I drop below five percent. Next, I will lose my arms and torso."

"Crap. Well, I'm not about to let an innocent clunker die on my watch. What do I do? How can I help?"

"Find anything with a battery. It's okay if it's damaged, as long as it still has power. Find whatever you can and bring it to me."

"Got it," he said, scurrying into the next room. "Don't worry, buddy. You can count on me."

The silence was chilling as Silas waited for the stranger to return. Would he return? Silas was not sure. Kindness had become so rare that it was hard to trust anyone. After a few minutes, his arms dropped and his body slouched. Now he had only his voice.

All hope was gone. The friendly stranger had left him. And of course he had. There was no reason for him to help. They had no prior relationship. It was foolish to think a human would help a simmi. By now he was probably half a mile away.

That was when his one eye caught sight of the duffel bag, which had slipped off his shoulder and plopped to the ground. One of the rifles was leaning against the desk as well. They were things the man would have taken if he had intended to leave.

Another chime came from his chest, filling the empty room with echoes.

Deacon reentered from a door in the back, dragging a simmi along with him. He gasped for air as he heaved the heavy body across the floor. The dead metal legs scraped the floor as he pulled the body closer and plopped it in front of Silas.

"Jeez, you clunkers are heavy. There are a whole bunch back in those cells. I nearly broke my back trying to bring two at once. Gave up halfway. You're lucky I didn't pass out from this one." He crouched beside Silas, who had slumped over, completely still. "Whoa, are you okay?"

"Hurry," Silas said. "Soon I will lose my voice and won't be able to instruct you."

Deacon hopped to his feet. "What do I do?"

"Retrieve the two wires from my bag."

Deacon looked down. The wires were sticking out of the top. He reached in and pulled them out, holding each end in front of Silas to show him. "Okay, now what?"

"There are two holes on the underside of my chest. They are color-coded with the wires."

Deacon leaned over and saw the holes. He sorted the wires and plugged them in.

"Now, remove the chest plate from the simmi."

Grabbing the thick metal plate from the dead simmi's chest, he yanked up with force. "It's screwed on pretty tight," he said, dropping it to the ground and looking back at Silas.

"There's a screwdriver in my bag. Hurry, we don't have much time."

"I'm going as fast as I can, buddy. Just hold on. I'm not letting you die." He rummaged through the bag. Hammer. Wrench. Pliers. Shears. Bolt cutters. Duct tape. Screwdriver. He held it up to show Silas. "I got it."

"Good, now unscrew the chest plate."

"Oh, right," Deacon said, as if he had forgotten why he needed the screwdriver in the first place. He loosened the plate and moved it aside. The battery occupied most of the space inside, with a small silicon chip sitting next to it. "Whoa, this stuff is rad."

"The battery should be color-coded as well. Clasp the wires on."

The moment they were connected, Silas could feel the energy flowing in.

Deacon watched with anticipation, as if he was waiting for something to happen. "Did I do it right? What now?"

"Now we wait," Silas responded.

"Really? That's a little disappointing. I was hoping for sparks or something. You know, something a little more exciting." He reached down to make sure the clips were secure. "Christ!" he yelled, pulling his hand back. "That thing is hot."

"Don't touch them. They heat up fast. Just stand back and wait. It will take some time."

"How long?"

"Overnight, maybe. If I power down, the process should be faster."

Deacon sat in one of the chairs. "Okay, then what am I supposed to do while we wait?"

"I don't expect you to wait for me. You may go as you please. All I ask is that you leave my tools."

"I'm not going anywhere. Not while Joe Cowboy and his goons are still out there." He swung his legs up onto the desk. "Besides, I need to finish the nap you so rudely interrupted."

"Very well. You should know, I can still see and hear while I'm powered down, so stay away from my bag."

Deacon raised his hands in the air. "Hey, I may be a thief, but my word is my word. I will not touch your stuff. *You* better not do any weird clunker stuff while *I'm* asleep. I should be the one with the trust issues here. You know, with clunkers attacking humanity and all."

"We're not all like that."

Deacon waved a dismissive hand. "Yeah, yeah. Just shut up and go to sleep, or power down, or whatever you call it." He leaned back with his arms crossed. "That oil sensor thing isn't going to go off all night, is it?"

"Not while I'm powered down."

"Good." He closed his eyes. "Maybe I can get a full night of rest for once."

Before powering down, Silas moved his head so he could see both Deacon and the front door. His one remaining eye would watch both with caution.

SCOUT'S PROMISE

WHEN SILAS POWERED up, Deacon was still in his chair, now whittling a stick with a pocket knife. He did not appear to be carving anything in particular. Just shaving away the time. The morning sun was beaming through the window and glistening off of the clean blade.

There was the familiar chime as Silas unfolded his legs to stand up. Deacon jumped in his seat, almost slicing his thumb as he grabbed for the edge of the desk to keep himself from falling.

"Jesus Christ!" he said, standing up himself. "You nearly gave me a heart attack." He dropped the half-sharpened stick and threw the knife in his pocket. "You all charged up now?"

Silas unplugged the wires from his chest. "Yes, I'm feeling much better." He unclamped the ends from the battery and placed the wires in his bag. "You're still here. I thought you would have left by now. Those men are not out there anymore."

"Yeah, well I wanted to make sure you were okay. It's not every day you come across a friendly clunker. Usually, whenever I see one of you guys, I'm looking down the barrel end of a gun. Clunkers can be dangerous if you aren't careful."

"What makes you think *I'm* not dangerous?"

"Please," Deacon said, circling around. "Just look at yourself. There's no way you were built for combat."

"I was built for companionship," Silas said, kneeling down to unscrew the head of the simmi he had drained.

"I hate to say it, but companionship's a luxury that died a long time ago. It's survival first."

With all of the screws undone, Silas separated the simmi's head from its body, placing it on the floor to his side.

"What I'm saying is," Deacon continued, "clunkers like you won't get very far if you stick to being friendly all the time. You got to look after yourself. Put everyone else second. They'll all leave you dead in the dirt."

Silas raised the screwdriver to his own neck and began to unscrew.

"Whoa!" Deacon said, reaching out to stop him. "What the hell are you doing?"

Silas pointed at his missing eye and torn up face. "My head is damaged. I'm replacing it."

A look of awe crept onto Deacon's face. "You can do that? You can just walk around willy-nilly without your head?"

"Yes. I won't be able to see, hear, or speak, but yes."

"How?"

Silas tapped his head. "Your brain is here, but mine is here." He lowered his hand to his chest. "Right next to my battery."

"You mean your chip."

"Correct. That's where my mind is stored."

"And your battery is your heart in this metaphor?"

"You could say that," he said, continuing to undo the screws.

"That's smart. You only have to protect one place. Why couldn't God be as smart as the guys at Limbys? If things were right in the world, I'd be able to pop off my head and stick on another, just like you." He tugged on his head in a comical fashion. "Nope. It's stuck on like a lid on a pickle jar. And if it does come off, pickle juice goes flying everywhere."

"Not every part is compatible with mine. In fact, most of them are not. Luckily, this one isn't military. It's some sort of service simmi. Not quite the same as me, but it has similar parts."

As Silas removed the last screw, Deacon stepped forward. "Do you need help there, buddy?"

"Yes, actually." He separated his head from his neck and held it up to expose the wires. "I would like you to unplug these for me. There should be four wires. Like I said before, once they're disconnected I won't be able to see, hear, or speak. I will need you to connect that other head. The same four wires go into the same four slots. Once I can see again, I'll do the rest."

Deacon nodded with enthusiasm. "Got it. Four wires out, four wires in. Easy enough." He widened his stance and raised his arms to grab the end of the first wire. "I'm ready when you are."

Silas tilted his head down to look at the man he was trusting to replace his head. Letting a stranger perform such a task was something Silas had never done before. Deacon was a self-proclaimed thief, but he had already helped with the battery, and he had not yet stolen his duffel bag.

"Okay," Silas said. "Go ahead. Disconnect them."

His vision went black. His hearing cut out. He was now at the mercy of a total stranger. After a moment of pure nothingness, he felt the weight of his disconnected head being removed from his hands. Deacon replaced it with a smaller, denser head. There was another moment of nothingness and then…

"—plug this in here," Deacon said. "Can you hear me, buddy?"

Silas tapped his finger twice to respond.

"Good. I had a feeling that one was your hearing. Three more to go and you're good as new. This one should be your sight."

A sea of colors filled Silas's eyes. Still holding his head up high, he could see the top of Deacon's greasy hair as he tinkered with the rest of the wires below.

"This one goes here," Deacon said, plugging in the third wire.

Silas regained control of his face. He could look around without turning his head. He had control of his neck and antennas as well.

"And the final wire goes here," Deacon said. He backed away and looked up at the new head. "How did I do?"

"You did well," Silas said, testing his voice. He lowered his arms to place the head on his shoulders.

Deacon slapped his leg with excitement. "You have to admit, I'm pretty good at this stuff."

"I was a little worried you would leave me headless." Silas reached for the screwdriver and tightened the screws around his neck.

"You, my friend, have trust issues, which is probably a good thing. Trusting people will get you killed. Most of the time, at least. You got lucky with me."

With his head fastened, Silas rolled it from side to side. "I appreciate your help, but I will be on my way now." He threw the screwdriver into his bag and slung the strap over his shoulder. "Good luck."

Deacon stepped in his way. "Wait. You said you're going to New Valley?"

"Yes, that's correct."

"I can come with you."

Silas stared at him with a puzzled curiosity. "Why?"

"No offense, but you'll never make it there on your own. You can't even shoot a gun, for Christ's sake. I'll be your personal bodyguard."

"What's in it for you?"

"New Valley is where Limbys is, right? I assume that's why you're going there." He pointed to the Limbys Technologies logo on Silas's chest. "To find other clunkers. Riley and the resistance are in New Valley. You know what that means, right?"

Silas shrugged.

"It means that's where all of the good stuff is. Guns. Ammo. Joe says they even have generators."

"It will be dangerous for you."

"Not any more dangerous than it is for *you*. Hell, we'll probably *both* be safer if we stick together. You can be our clunker diplomat, and I can shoot our way through if diplomacy fails."

"I'm not much of a diplomat. They don't really listen to me."

Deacon shrugged. "Hey, we all have our flaws. Don't beat yourself up about it. You can't fight, and you can't negotiate. My point is, you won't last on your own. I've only known you for a few hours and I've already saved you twice. You have nothing to lose and everything to gain."

It was true, Silas was better off with a partner. The man had already proven himself twice. He had killed the men outside the church and had helped recharge his battery. Silas nodded. "Okay. You can come."

"Great!" Deacon cheered. "Of course, I would have come even if you weren't okay with it. It's not like you could do anything about it. But this is a much better arrangement. Mutual cooperation is the best kind." He stuck his hand out. "You already know my name, but what's yours?"

Silas accepted his handshake. "My name is Silas."

"Well, Silas, I solemnly swear to protect you from danger. Scout's promise."

Another chime rang.

"But before we go anywhere," he tapped Silas's chest, "we're going to take care of your little oil situation. That noise is going to get us killed."

Dumb Luck

THE TWO STROLLED along the street, Deacon with his two rifles and Silas with the duffel bag. The sun had climbed up to its peak, beating down on the hot asphalt.

Drops of sweat trickled from Deacon's face. He wiped his forehead and turned to Silas. "So, where do you usually find oil? Where do we start?"

"There are a few places we can look." He pointed to the abandoned cars scattered throughout the road. "Some of these vehicles may have oil. Most are probably dry, but occasionally you get lucky."

Deacon stared at Silas, waiting for him to continue. "Okay, so what's the better way? I don't want to be out here all day."

"Unfortunately, if we want oil, we may have to spend an entire day looking. It's become a rare commodity."

Another chime sounded off.

"And you've had to listen to that goddamn thing the whole time?"

"Yes, I have."

"Jeez. I don't know how you put up with it. I've only been with you for a few hours and the sound's already driving me nuts. Any longer and I may have to blow my brains out. After that, you're on your own."

Silas ignored what he could only assume to be a joke. "Our other option is to search these stores. Most of them are empty, but we could get—"

"Lucky," Deacon said, finishing Silas's thought. "So, we're just going to stumble around and wait for dumb luck. That's the plan."

"There's not much else we can do," Silas said. He pointed to the store on the right. "We can start there and work our way down the block."

"This is stupid," Deacon said, following him into the store. "There has to be a better way."

They rummaged through, finding nothing but useless toys. The place was filled with dolls, action figures, and other things that served no purpose in a post-war life. A miniature train track ran along the perimeter of the room, ramping up and over the entrance and continuing along a shelf. The caboose of a plastic train now dangled from a ledge after crashing into a dollhouse that had been placed in its way.

Deacon grabbed a green plastic army man and held it up with a wide smile. "Man, I loved these things when I was a kid." He reached for another one and moved them in a playful manner. "Reporting for duty," he said, moving one of the figures to the rhythm of his voice. "What are my orders?" He responded to himself with the other figure in a slightly lower voice. "I want you to go out there and rip them apart, soldier. Show them that green plastic is the best plastic. We must defend green at all costs. No matter what the consequences. Those reds and blues don't stand a chance." He slammed both figures down in unison. "Yes, sir!"

Silas stared, saying nothing.

"What?" Deacon said, looking back. "You've never seen a grown man play with toys before?"

Silas shook his head.

"Well, get used to it. I may look old, but I'm still a big baby at heart." He put down the two army men and moved his attention to a toy car, rolling its wheels along the flat surface and making car noises with his mouth.

Silas picked up a toy version of a simmi. It was packaged in a cardboard box with a thin plastic display film. The figure resembled a military model. It was tall and bulky with a blue stripe across its chest. The back of the box had a stylized cartoon of the blue-striped simmi. In one hand the simmi held an oversized gun. With the other, he pointed out toward the customer. A white dialogue bubble floated over its head. *We protect you.* The Limbys logo sat in the bottom corner.

He placed the box down and grabbed a smaller one next to it. This one held the figure of a household model and had a shocking resemblance to Silas. Sleek and friendly. On the back was another cartoon. This one showed the household simmi kneeling beside a golden retriever. The simmi used one hand to pet the dog and the other to give a thumbs-up to the customer. There was another dialogue bubble. *We serve you.*

Another chime.

Deacon put down the toy car and looked over at Silas. "Why does that thing beep for oil, but not for your battery?"

Silas placed the toy back down and continued to walk down the aisle. "There used to be a sound for my battery. It just stopped working."

"Probably a blessing in disguise. Dare I say, dumb luck."

Gunfire echoed in short bursts outside. They both turned, ready and alert. Silas followed Deacon to the window and peered into the street. At first, he saw nothing. Just the same ghost town as before. Another burst of fire revealed a bright muzzle flash reflecting off a cracked windshield.

"Over there," Silas whispered, pointing in the direction of the flash.

Deacon squinted. "I can barely see from here. Let's get closer." He hopped through the door and spun his back against a car.

"Wait!" Silas said. "It's dangerous."

"I'll be fine. I just want to get a better look. I don't have brand-new clunker eyes like you." He turned the corner, out of Silas's view.

There were a few more bursts, and then the gunfire stopped. Silas continued to watch from the window, waiting for the threat to go away. Waiting for Deacon to return. Waiting for the problem to solve itself. But would it solve itself? Probably not. If anything, his new bodyguard would get himself killed.

He was considering stepping out to help when Deacon returned, trotting back to the store.

"Guess what," he said, rubbing his palms together. "Today's your lucky day, buddy. There's a group of clunkers, and they've got a whole stockpile of oil. It's a fortress of greasy goodness."

Silas did not share the same enthusiasm. "If the oil is guarded, how do we get it?"

"Guarded? Weren't you listening? They're clunkers. Just go up and ask for some."

"It doesn't work like that. I can't just ask for oil."

"Sure you can. You just have to be confident."

"It won't work," Silas repeated. "You're supposed to protect me, not send me into danger."

"It's dangerous for me, but not for you." He grabbed Silas's arm and led him out of the store. "Just go on and get your oil. We've already wasted plenty of time. You do want to get to New Valley, right?"

Silas stumbled into the street and caught sight of the squad of simmies. It was the same group from earlier. Red Stripe, Dented Chest, Dirt Smudge, and a whole bunch of others. Red Stripe was in a fit of laughter.

"See?" Deacon said. "That one's in a good mood. Just go up and join them."

Silas found himself fighting instinct, walking toward the group of simmies despite his body urging him not to. It was as if Deacon's words had burrowed into his mind, driving him toward a clear and present danger.

As he walked forward, he could see why Red Stripe was laughing. There were four bodies at his feet, two men and two women, and fresh spurts of blood in the dirt.

He stopped in his tracks as fear took over. In one swift motion, he spun around and walked away. Deacon, who was watching from the store, shook his head and mouthed something with his lips. Silas couldn't make out the words, but it didn't matter. There was nothing Deacon could say to convince him to turn back. He would return to safety, and they would continue searching the stores.

His oil gauge chimed. He froze.

The blaring sound prompted Deacon to duck behind a car. Silas prayed that the others hadn't heard the obvious noise. He began to tiptoe forward but was stopped by the familiar grating voice.

"Hey, you!" Red Stripe yelled. "Stop right there."

Silas obeyed but did not turn around.

"Are you spying on us?"

His mind was too jumbled to form words. What had he gotten himself into? Why had he listened to someone he just met?

"Hey!" Red Stripe hollered. "I'm talking to you."

Silas was still too frightened to speak.

"Turn around!"

With his hands raised, Silas slowly turned his body to face the simmies.

"Come over here," Red Stripe commanded.

Dirt Smudge pointed at Silas's chest. "The pink heart. It's the runt from last night."

After a long look at the painted heart, Red Stripe locked eyes with Silas. "I thought I told you not to follow us, runt."

"I...uh, I'm sorry. I didn't mean to follow you. I just happened to cross your path."

Red Stripe stepped back and bellowed with laughter. "Look at how scared he is. I sure made an impression on this little guy last night, huh, boys?"

The rest joined in, pointing at the defeated simmi and imitating his frail posture.

Silas lowered his head. "I really am sorry," he said, backing away. "It won't happen again."

Red Stripe grabbed his shoulder and pulled him back. "Now hold on there, runt. There must be a good reason you decided to approach us again. Is there something you want?"

Silas eyed the stack of oil.

"Oil," Red Stripe said, following Silas's gaze. "You want oil. But I already told you. That oil's not for you."

"I just need one jug," Silas said in the most confident voice he could fake.

He made eye contact, holding his gaze for as long as he could. Unfazed, Red Stripe leaned forward to match his stare. Silas turned away and stumbled back, but Red Stripe pulled him in closer, snickering in his face. "Did you just try to stare me down?" He turned to the others. "Can you believe that, boys? The runt tried to stare me down." They hollered with uncontrollable laughter. "You know, I'm starting to like you. I'll tell you what." He walked to the stack of oil and grabbed a jug from the top. "I can't give you an entire jug, but I'll give you a taste. Fair enough?"

Silas was flustered by the sudden generosity. Was Deacon right? Was a little bit of confidence all he needed to get what he wanted?

"I'll take your silence as a thank you," Red Stripe said, twisting off the nozzle. "Now, where should I pour it?"

Silas pointed to his shoulder, where the cap for his oil tank was, but Red Stripe ignored him and instead raised the jug over Silas's head. He flipped the jug over and poured a steady stream of slick fluid onto Silas's face. The oil coated his entire body, dripping down to the soles of his feet. When the jug was empty, Red Stripe tossed it aside. The plastic bounced off the hood of a car and onto the ground.

"Oops," he said, chuckling to himself. "I guess that was more than a taste, huh?"

Again, the others busted out laughing. They hooted and hollered and cooed and cackled.

Humiliated, it was now clear that Silas would not get oil. To stay any longer would be pointless. He took a step back, praying that they were all too distracted to notice. He took another. And then another. And then…

"Hey!" Dirt Smudge yelled. "That little fleshball is taking our oil!"

Silas turned to see Deacon crouched behind the cart holding two jugs, one in each hand.

"Run!" he yelled to Silas, sprinting away.

As the simmies raised their guns, Silas spun around to follow Deacon. He kept his eyes on the bright red jugs as he bobbed and weaved through rows of cars. Gunfire rattled from behind. Shards of smashed windshields flew into the air. A bullet nicked Silas's shoulder. Another grazed his thigh. He ignored both and kept running.

"Hold your fire!" Red Stripe yelled. The gunfire ceased immediately. "They're not worth our time. We're late enough as it is."

There were no more bullets, but Silas still found himself ducking his head as he ran. A few blocks down, Deacon had stopped in front of a burger joint, resting on their outdoor patio. He sat at an old wooden table with long benches on either side and a torn umbrella poking up from the middle. The umbrella had an image of an astronaut holding a burger on his open palm. Underneath was the name of the joint, Space Taste. The two jugs that Deacon had stolen were sitting on the table.

"How's that for dumb luck?" Deacon said, handing one of the jugs to Silas.

"It certainly could have gone better."

"Hey, we're both alive and we got what we came for. If that's not a success, then I don't know what is."

"I told you asking wouldn't work."

"And I told *you* that you need to be more confident. What happened back there was a joke, and a pretty hilarious one at that."

"A joke?"

"Yeah. Watching you try to assert yourself. I can tell it doesn't come easy for you. That much is crystal clear."

"I didn't think it was very funny," Silas said, placing the jugs on the ground. "It was humiliating."

Deacon waved his hand. "Ah, quit being a baby. The world's died ten times over. No one cares if you embarrass yourself a little."

The familiar chime rang out.

Deacon pointed to the jug on the ground. "What are you waiting for? I didn't just steal that as a souvenir."

Silas picked it up and unscrewed the top. "I fill up and then we go to New Valley. You're still coming, right?"

"Of course I'm still coming. Nothing's changed. A clunker like you doesn't stand a chance on your own."

"Could you please stop saying *clunker*?" Silas said, pouring a steady flow of oil into his tank. "That term is a bit derogatory."

"What do you prefer?"

"Simulated intelligence is better. Simmi is fine as well."

Deacon tilted his head. "Really? You prefer simulated intelligence? To me, that's much worse than clunker. It means your intelligence isn't real. Isn't that the reason the war started in the first place? You know, equal rights and everything? I've come across a lot of clunkers, and if there's one thing I've learned, it's that they're intelligent. Hell, I'd go as far as to say that clunkers are smarter than eighty percent of the human population. That is, back when there *was* a human population. Now it's probably around sixty. All the dummies died out."

Silas lowered the half-emptied jug and secured the cap. "I respect the name they gave us."

Deacon shrugged. "I guess I just don't understand." He smirked. "What about robot?"

Silas flinched at the term. "That's just as bad as clunker."

"Yeah, I know. I'm just joking around."

"It's not something to joke about. Robots are what you find in factories. On assembly lines doing programmed work. They can't think for themselves. Calling a simmi a robot is like calling a human a garden gnome."

"Yeah, I'm just messing with you," Deacon said, glancing at the red jug in Silas's hand. "Are you all set with the oil? Ready to go?"

"Yes," Silas answered, reaching for the other jug. "But we should take a different route. Those simmies said they're also going to New Valley. We should stay out of their way."

Deacon chuckled. "You really are terrified of them, aren't you? Fine by me." He pointed down the intersecting road. "We'll take this street and head for the woods. Get away from town. That'll keep us safe from the clunkers."

"Simmi," Silas insisted.

"I'll call *you* simmi, but I ain't got an inch of respect for those other hunks of metal. I'm calling them clunkers."

BEAR CANISTER

THE LATE SUMMER sun shined a blinding ray of light off of Silas's chest plate and into Deacon's eyes.

"Jeez," Deacon said, turning away. "Do you have to be so damn shiny all the time?"

Silas walked along the dirt path without looking over. "If it bothers you, walk over there."

"You know," Deacon said, pointing a playful finger at his new companion. "This is exactly why people don't like clunkers. Always telling you what to do. I'll walk where I want to walk." He moved to the other side. "I'm walking over here because I want to. Not because you told me to."

"What are you even talking about? Are you going to be like this the entire way?"

"It's what you signed up for. This bodyguard comes complete with unabridged commentary. Nothing's been cut, not even the dumb stuff."

"As long as we make it to New Valley, I suppose you can say whatever you want."

"Words you'll regret, my friend. You have no idea what kind of nonsense I'm capable of. They say it's my strongest feature. It's why everyone hates me so much." He shot a wink. "But you don't hate me. I can tell."

"What do you mean, you can tell?"

"You're still around. You haven't run off yet. I know you're just using me to get where you need to go, but still, at some point you have to weigh your options. Get to your destination safely or ditch me on the way there. You haven't hit that wall yet, so I'm still in the clear." He pumped out an enthusiastic thumbs-up.

Silas glanced at his thumb in silence and then turned back to the trail.

"You're a simmi of few words. I can't say I didn't expect that. You sure do have your eyes on the prize. What do you expect to find there anyway? In New Valley, I mean."

"Others like me…a home…a place to belong."

"Aren't we all? Unfortunately, there will be no home for *me* in New Valley."

"You don't have to come. I'll find a way on my own."

"No, I'm coming. I want to see Limbys. I want to witness the incredible genius of a company that singlehandedly ended the world."

"They singlehandedly started mine. Without Limbys Technologies, I wouldn't exist."

"I'm not blaming the war on *all* clunkers," Deacon said. "Obviously, some of you just got caught up in the whole situation, but you have to admit, if you guys were never created, there would still be a whole lot of us left."

"From what I understand, humans were already headed down this path. Simulated intelligence just acted as a catalyst."

Deacon paused for a moment to reflect, and then nodded. "You know what? You're probably right. We have a bad track record of screwing ourselves over. You could say it's our one defining trait."

"Do you think—"

"Hold on," Deacon said, cutting him off. "Look."

He pointed to a large camouflaged tent. Its colors were hidden in the dull greens and browns of the forest. Long poles arched over the canopy and anchored into the ground. The open flap in the front wavered in the wind.

Looking beyond the tent, they noticed several others. It was an entire campsite concealed by nature. Vines and ivy entangled the seemingly abandoned settlement. In the center, there was a modest fire pit filled with dark coals and white ash.

Deacon brought a finger to his lips as a signal of silence and then stepped toward the camp. Silas grabbed his shoulder and held him back.

"What are you doing?" he asked in the quietest voice he could manage. "It's dangerous. Let's just go around."

Deacon shook his hand off. "I don't see anyone around, and there's probably some good stuff in these tents."

"Someone could be coming back."

"Look," Deacon said, turning around to face Silas. "You may have been able to survive this long by staying away from people, but you and I are different. I need more than a just quick charge from a dead clunker. If they have food or weapons, I fully intend on stealing them. That's how I've survived up until now, and I don't plan on changing my ways to appease some simmi I just met. If you have a problem with that, you can just head on over to New Valley on your own. Do you understand?"

Silas nodded and reluctantly followed his lead into camp. They crept closer, staying low and minding their steps. With care, Deacon held out one of his rifles. Silas placed the oil jugs on the ground and accepted the weapon.

They stood in front of the first tent, watching the unzipped flap wave in the wind. If the tent was occupied, there would be a struggle and someone would die. Silas tightened his grip on the barrel of his rifle. If such a struggle were to break out, would he be any help? His new friend seemed to think so.

An uncomfortable tension grew as Deacon reached forward to grab the flap. In one fluid motion, he ripped it open and charged inside with crazed eyes. Silas moved out of the way, expecting to hear some sort of struggle.

There was no struggle, and after only a short moment, Deacon fell out of the tent, shaking his head and gasping for air. He stumbled over to the nearest tree and leaned against its trunk. A look of nausea had invaded his usual cheery face. His skin was pale and coated with a slimy layer of oil.

Silas trotted over, placing a hand on Deacon's arched back and leaning in to see his bloodshot eyes. "Are you okay?"

"Christ!" Deacon hollered. "It's a nightmare in there."

The tent remained wide open. Silas turned to see the sight of two bodies, lying side by side near the back of the tent. Rotting flesh, deep red blood, and feeding maggots all worked together to create a horrific scene.

He turned away, unable to bear the sight, and focused again on Deacon, who had just finished vomiting.

"Feel better now?" he whispered.

"Much better now that I've puked my brains out. And you don't have to whisper. There's no one around."

"What about the other tents?"

"They're all either empty or full of corpses."

"How do you know?"

"Why would anyone just leave a couple of dead bodies to rot in a hotbox next to their camp? If anything, they would have buried the bodies, or burned them, or at least dragged them away."

"Maybe they just don't like handling dead bodies," Silas said, still whispering.

"Hey!" Deacon yelled to the other tents. "Anybody there? Come out now or we'll...I don't know...we'll hurt you!"

They waited for a response, but there was none.

"See?" Deacon said. "It's settled. There's no one around."

"You need to work on your threats," Silas said, walking back to retrieve his oil.

"Ouch," Deacon said, stepping back from the puke-covered tree and walking to the center of the campsite. "That hurts coming from someone like you."

Silas joined him by the fire pit and stared at the black coals. "Those two in the tent are military. This must have been an outpost of some kind."

"What makes you say that?"

"You didn't notice their uniforms?"

"I was little too focused on the horrible smell to notice what they were wearing."

Silas tapped the front of his face, where a nose would be if he were human. "I can't smell."

Deacon grinned. "Right. How about you put that handicap to use and check out those other tents? We should look for anything worth taking, but I don't know if I can stomach another tent of human stew."

Silas glanced around the campsite. "You're sure there's no one around?"

"Quit stalling. You're so paranoid."

After rummaging through the tents, Silas returned with an armful of boxes. Deacon was sitting at a small wooden picnic table.

"Hey, Silas!" Deacon hollered. "Look what I found." He held up a clear container that was made of thick plastic.

Silas stared at the object. "You found an empty bottle?"

"It's not a bottle. It's a bear canister. It was just lying on the ground over there."

"Bear canister?" Silas repeated, leaning closer to examine its cylindrical shape.

"Yeah, it's for camping. You put food inside, and it keeps the bears from getting it. We used them all the time when I was a kid."

"It looks like a big plastic water bottle to me."

"Maybe to the untrained eye, but trust me, this thing is gold. Look." He twisted off the lid with a surprising amount of excitement. "It's airtight. It traps in the scent, so bears don't smell your grub."

"Or you could keep water in it," Silas said. "Like a water bottle."

"Well, yeah, but that would be a waste. I don't think you realize the full potential of this product." He held it up to Silas's face. "Look."

Silas stared at the empty container and shrugged. "I'll take your word for it."

"I guess as someone who doesn't eat, you wouldn't understand." He placed the bear canister back on the table and glanced at the clutter of boxes in Silas's arms. "Speaking of food, it looks like you found some goodies."

Silas dumped them on the table.

Deacon picked one up and read the label. "Meal, Ready-to-Eat. You know, I've heard these things aren't bad." He flipped it over to read the back. "Jambalaya. That actually sounds pretty damn appetizing." He ripped open the box and found several smaller packages inside. The one labeled *MRE Heater* had a warning printed near the bottom. He held it up and read out loud.

"Warning—One: The vapors released by an activated heater contain hydrogen, a flammable gas. Do not use near an open flame. Two: The vapors released by an activated heater can displace oxygen. Do not use in a confined space. Three: Keep away from children." He skipped down to the instructions, this time only reading to himself. "Making this stuff is complicated. I guess the days of sticking a pizza in the microwave are long gone."

Silas picked up his own box to examine it. "How do you make it?"

"We need water. Do you have any water?"

Silas pointed to the canteen around Deacon's shoulder. "No, but you do."

"Oh, right," Deacon said, reaching for his canteen. "You're a simmi. You don't drink."

He grabbed the pouch that was supposedly filled with jambalaya and placed it in the MRE heater. Then, he poured in a trickle of water and sealed the top. The bag hissed as the water mixed with the powdery substance at the bottom of the heater.

"Now we place it back in the box and—Ow!" He yelled, dropping the bag on the table. "Damn, that thing got hot fast." He picked up the empty box and scooped the sealed heater inside. "Now we wait," he said, setting the box down. "Did you find anything else?"

"There are some scarecrows over there," Silas said, pointing beyond the tents.

"Scarecrows? In the middle of the forest?"

Silas shrugged. "Strange, I know."

Deacon poked at the box of jambalaya. "We've got time to kill while we wait for this stuff to cook. Let's go check it out. But first..." He opened the bear canister, tossed the sizzling box inside, and sealed the lid shut. "See? Now bears can't get any of my tasty jambalaya. This thing is already coming in handy. Now, take me to these scarecrows you speak of."

Silas led him to a clearing behind the tents. At the far end, there were four scarecrows mounted on wooden frames. Pictures of simmies were attached to the heads.

"Ah," Deacon said with delight. "For a second I thought you were pulling my leg. This, my friend, is a firing range. They must have been training out here. Either that, or they just got bored and wanted to shoot something. And apparently, there was some sort of disagreement in the group." He pointed to the ground in front of the scarecrows. There were six bodies sprawled in a circle, each peppered with multiple bullet wounds. He stepped closer with his hands perched on his hips. "Now this looks like there was a good old-fashioned Mexican standoff."

"Mexican standoff?" Silas asked.

"Don't tell me you've never heard of a Mexican standoff."

Silas shrugged and shook his head.

"Haven't you seen any Westerns? You know, cowboys, horses, six-shooters?"

"I've heard of them, but no, I've never seen a Western film. Most of the movies I've seen are animated."

"You mean you've never seen the classics?"

"There are plenty of animated classics."

"Yeah, sure, but you've never seen *A Fistful of Dollars, The Magnificent Seven, High Noon, The Wild Bunch*. You know, the classics."

"No, I haven't."

"Well," Deacon said, standing over one of the bodies and pulling out his very own six-shooter. "This is a Mexican standoff." He dramatically pointed his gun at nothing. "Freeze! Don't move!"

He trotted over to where he was aiming, spun around, and aimed back at where he was. "It's you who needs to cool your horses, fella. I ain't afraid of shootin'."

He shimmied to a third spot. "That's right. If you shoot him, I shoot you. Simple as that."

A fourth spot. "How's this for simple? Why don't I just shoot all of y'all."

He raced to a fifth spot and this time lowered his gun. "Let's all just take it easy now. Nobody has to die today."

In one quick motion, he sprung his revolver back up. "Bang!" he yelled. His voice echoed through the woods. "And then everyone's dead. That's usually how Mexican standoffs end. A whole bunch of dead bodies. Sometimes there's one lucky sucker who gets out alive."

Silas watched from the side, impressed by Deacon's performance. "What's the point, if everyone just ends up dead? Nothing is accomplished."

"That's because people are stubborn. Everyone wants what they want, and nobody's willing to compromise. They can't afford to compromise."

"Why not? Diplomacy is always the better option."

"Times are desperate. In a lot of cases, if you don't keep everything for yourself, you die. If someone survives a shootout, they reap the rewards. If no one survives, it's scavengers like us who reap the rewards. In this case, the reward happens to be some tasty jambalaya." He looked back toward camp, and then at the four scarecrows. "We probably have a little more time. Want to shoot a few rounds?"

Silas glanced at the picture attached to one of the straw heads. It was the same drawing he had found on the back of the simmi toy box, with the same text printed below. *We protect you.* "I think I'll pass."

"Ah, come on. Is it the pictures that bother you?" He tore them off. "There, is that better?"

"Really, I would rather not."

"I've seen how you handle a gun. You need the practice. If we're going to New Valley together, you need to have my back."

Silas stared at the four scarecrows.

"I'm not taking no for an answer," Deacon said, holding out the six-shooter. "You're going to have to shoot me to shut me up."

Silas took the gun and examined the cylinder. "Where did you get this?"

"Where do you think? I stole it from our good friend, Joe Cowboy, of course. He really goes the extra mile with the whole cowboy getup. You have to admire the guy's dedication. I snagged plenty of ammo, too. It's probably one of the reasons he hates me so much."

"One of many, I presume."

"Right you are," Deacon said, snapping his fingers and pointing back. "Now, let's see some shooting. Just pretend like you're in your own little Mexican standoff, and these four lovely scarecrows are ready to shoot back."

"Fine, I'll shoot one round," Silas said, widening his stance.

"Great! I'll watch closely and give you pointers."

With the gun at his waist, Silas waited for Deacon to give some sort of cue.

Deacon nodded. "Whenever you're ready."

Before he could blink, four loud cracks burst out in succession. A flock of nearby birds took flight as the sharp sound cut through the forest. The smoking barrel of the gun was pointed at the head of the last target, and there was a perfectly placed hole in the center of all four scarecrows.

Deacon's jaw hung open. He rubbed his eyes and ran up to the targets to look at the holes.

"Jesus Christ!" he yelled. His voice cracked midsentence. He pressed his eye against the newly formed bullet hole and peered through to the other side. "You didn't tell me you could do that. You're like the reincarnation of Clint Eastwood."

Silas lowered the six-shooter. "Who?"

"Man, you really need to watch some Westerns." He stepped away from the target to look back at Silas. "Why in the world didn't you shoot like that when Joe and his goons were trying to kill us back in the RV?"

"I don't know."

"You don't know?" He threw his arms up. "What do you mean you don't know? That is the best shooting I've seen in my life. You could have wiped them out."

Silas shrugged. "Shooting is simple. It's all about the angle. Simple geometry. Like mini golf. All you have to do is plan out your shot, aim, and execute. But if someone's shooting back, it's different. I panic."

"Well, we're going to work on that, because with that kind of shooting, we're unstoppable."

"Other simmies can do the same thing. Military models can shoot better and faster."

Deacon took the revolver back and patted Silas on the back. "Have some confidence, man. How many times do I have to say that? Sure, they're designed to kill and you're designed to hug, but that doesn't mean you're not a total badass."

"No one's ever called me that before."

"What, a badass? Well, that's what you are, my friend. Keep that in mind the next time we're in a pickle."

"I told you. I can't shoot under pressure."

"Quit it, will you? Of course you can. Like you said, all you have to do is plan, aim, and execute. It's as simple as that."

A loud pop came from the campsite. Deacon and Silas dropped to the ground.

"Crap," Deacon said. "Is someone back at the camp?"

"There must be, and they're shooting at something."

"Trigger happy. That's never a good thing."

"Let's just leave," Silas said. "We don't need to go back."

"All of that food is there."

Silas started to back away. "We can find more somewhere else. It's too dangerous to go back."

"Dangerous? I just learned I have the most badass simmi on my side. I think we'll be fine."

Deacon trotted off, leaving Silas alone in the middle of the deserted shooting range. Deacon seemed to attract danger, but Silas knew he wouldn't get far without him. He certainly wouldn't reach New Valley on his own. With Deacon, he stood a chance. Fighting his instinct to flee, he forced himself to follow Deacon toward the sound of danger.

Deacon was already out of sight. Silas slowed down as he approached the camp. When he saw the first tent, he crouched behind the nearest bush and listened for their intruder. At first, he heard nothing.

"Son of a bitch," Deacon. "Silas, are you back there? You can come out. There's no one here."

Silas emerged from his hiding spot.

"I guess these things aren't as airtight as I thought." He held up the bear canister. There was a gaping hole in the side. The plastic had warped, as if a grenade had gone off inside.

Deacon twisted the cap off. "The lid did its job. It's the side that blew out." He reached through the hole and pulled out the Meal, Ready-to-Eat. The box was perfectly intact.

"The thing's still warm," he said, removing the heater pouch and reading the warnings again. "The vapors released by an activated heater can displace oxygen. I guess we should have paid more attention to that one. There must have been a ton of pressure to do this kind of damage."

"You can make another, if you still want to try one," Silas said, pointing to the pile of MREs on the table. "There are plenty left."

"No need. The bear canister may be ruined, but the food's still good." He opened the heater and removed the inner pouch. "Man, I haven't had a hot meal in ages." He ripped off the top and stuck his nose in. "It doesn't smell half bad."

He tilted his head back and shoveled the sludge into his mouth until his cheeks were puffed out. As he chewed, the look on his face turned from curious optimism to instant regret.

He tried to speak, but a dribble of sauce oozed out. His gullet bobbed in and out as he tried to swallow the food. Tears pooled in his eyes. Another attempt to swallow prompted a sudden coughing fit. He turned away and let the sludge fall from his mouth.

After spewing out the vile slime, he wiped his mouth and turned to Silas. "That has to be the most horrid thing I've ever eaten. It's like vomit in a box. Do we really make soldiers eat this trash?" He grabbed his canteen to wash out the taste. "Leave the rest. I can't stomach another bite."

Silas glanced at the pile of boxes. "That's a waste, don't you think? Food is food."

"Food may be food, but *this* isn't food."

"But we have no other food. We should take what we can."

Deacon took another swig of water. "You can take them if you want, but I'm not going to eat them."

Silas scooped the boxes into his bag. "You say that now, but you'll thank me later."

"I'm telling you, it's a waste of space, but whatever makes you happy. Now, come on. Let's get moving.

There's nothing else left for us here." He grabbed the blown-out bear canister, tossed it into the ash-filled fire pit, and walked into the forest.

BAIT

THE FOREST GREW denser as they continued their journey to New Valley. The grass was taller, and the flowers were more vibrant than ever. The trees embraced the warm sun. Their branches swayed in the summer breeze, and their roots dug deep into the healthy soil.

"That's when the guy jumped me," Deacon said, concluding a longwinded story. "He tackled me to the ground and started swinging. Punch after punch. He just wouldn't stop. I don't know what I did to set him off, but at that point, there was just no reasoning with the guy."

In the distance, Silas heard the faint sound of bells. Windchimes. Or was it nothing? Deacon didn't seem to hear it.

He ignored the sound and focused back on Deacon's story. "You don't know why he attacked you?"

"Not a clue. It baffles me to this day. That kind of thing makes you wonder just how many crazies there are out there."

"So what did you do?"

"The only thing I could do. I took the beating as best I could."

"You didn't fight back?"

"Hey, I'm all for standing up for yourself, but the man had a knife. You've got to be smart in situations like that. Punching back might have gotten me killed. So, I took the beating of a lifetime. That's how I got this." He pointed to his upper cheek.

Silas glanced at the scar that he had somehow missed until now. "That's quite the scar."

"Yes, it is. Lucky for me, I'm pretty good at taking a beating. Eventually, the idiot got tired. He wasn't exactly an athlete. He had worked himself into such a frenzy that after only a few seconds he was lying on the ground next to me. I got up, stood over him, and clocked him right in the nose. He was out just like that." Deacon snapped his fingers. "Turned off like a light bulb. And while he was out, I grabbed his stuff and ran. Takers keepers, right? I still have his knife." He pulled out his pocketknife.

Again, the sound of windchimes rang. This time it was louder. Silas swiveled his head to find where it was coming from. It seemed to be from every direction. Deacon still did not seem to hear it.

Silas shook his head and turned back to the knife. "How long have you had it?"

Deacon rubbed his chin. "Let's see. The guy attacked me right after the riots started. That would make it…nine years? I rarely use it. Threatened a couple people, but guns are usually more effective." He slipped the knife back into his pocket and held up his rifle. "I mean, what scares you more? A dinky little knife or this bad boy?"

"They're both pretty frightening to me. The rifle is louder, but the knife has an unsettling intimacy."

"I can appreciate that. From my experience, it's usually not the weapon that scares me, but the person behind it. The right kind of lunatic could make a feather terrifying. It would be difficult, but they would find a way."

Once more, the bells rang. They had grown to a volume that was impossible to ignore. "Do you hear that—" Silas started to ask, but he paused at the sight of the clearing in front of them.

"Whoa," Deacon muttered, staring ahead.

There was a circular area absent of trees. In the center, a lone lifeless simmi was slouched on its knees. Hanging from the surrounding branches were dozens of windchimes. Every time the wind blew, a medley of bells rang throughout the forest.

"Well, that's not eerie at all," Deacon said. "One lonely clunker praying in the middle of a field surrounded by bells." He glanced up at the nearest tree to study one of the chimes. "Why in the world would those be up there?"

"Look," Silas said, pointing. "Oil."

Next to the simmi was a black jug, presumably filled with oil. The simmi had propped its limp hand on top, but the cap remained unturned.

"Is the clunker dead?" Deacon said, raising his arm to block the sun. "Hey! Are you dead?"

"Don't yell. You might wake it up."

"I don't think it *can* wake up. I'm pretty sure it's dead."

"How do you know?"

Deacon plucked a rock from the ground. "There's only one way to find out."

Before Silas could stop him, he tossed the rock into the air. It arched over the clear field and hit the simmi in the head. Its neck cocked to the side and its head fell forward.

"Yup," Deacon confirmed. "The thing is definitely dead."

"That means the oil is ours," Silas said, holding up his nearly empty red jugs. "Good timing. We're almost out." He stepped forward, into the clearing.

Deacon studied the clearing more closely. There was no grass. Up until now, most of the grass had reached their knees. "Why isn't there any grass?" he asked himself, watching Silas walk further into the clearing. "It's like someone dug it up and didn't bother to regrow it."

At that moment, it hit him. He realized what was wrong. The chimes. The oil. The clunker. "Wait, Silas! Stop!"

Silas dropped like a sack of beans, falling to his knees. An incredible force pulled his arms down, and his legs locked in place. He collapsed forward, overwhelmed by the growing weight of his own body.

A grainy distortion concealed his attempts to speak. His mind was scrambled. His perception of the world was cut into snippets. Time no longer had meaning. How long had he been on the ground? Where was he? Would this feeling ever stop? The sensation grew more intense until it was unbearable, and then it grew some more.

And then all at once, it was gone. The extra weight. The downward pull. The spiraling path toward insanity. It was all gone in an instant. He pressed his hand to his chest and then pushed off the ground to stand up.

"Are you all right there, buddy?" Deacon asked, trotting over to help.

Silas focused on planting his feet on the ground, and then looked at Deacon. "I don't know what happened."

Deacon kicked away the grassless soil to reveal a thick layer of metal plating buried underneath. "It's an electromagnet," he said. "You walked right into a trap for clunkers."

"How?" Silas said, still disoriented.

"Someone must have buried it. I found a wire leading over there." He pointed beyond some bushes. "It connects to a generator on the other side."

"Who would bury a magnet like this?"

Deacon shrugged. "Beats me. Someone who has a problem with clunkers is my guess. But that doesn't really narrow it down." He crouched and used his hands to push aside more soil. "Whoever it was, they went through a lot of work to hide this magnet. A hole this size would take days to dig. Weeks even."

Silas looked at the lifeless simmi that was still kneeling by the oil jug. If his experience was at all similar to what Silas had gone through, he had died both scared and confused.

"You're lucky I was here to shut it off," Deacon said. He knelt in front of the metal body, glaring into the dead simmi's eyes. "Or else you'd be like this guy. Caught like a rabbit in a snare trap. Are you damaged at all?"

"I don't believe so. Although, my power level is low. Twenty-seven percent. You mentioned a generator?"

"Yeah, just past those bushes. Follow me."

Silas brushed the simmi's hand aside, grabbed the oil jug, and then followed Deacon.

"You know," Deacon said, "your battery doesn't last very long. I've seen clunkers last twice as long without a charge."

Silas tapped his chest. "It's old. My battery, that is. Years of recharging have worn it out."

"Why don't you replace it? We've seen plenty of dead clunkers with batteries for you to take."

"I could, but it would require a full shutdown of my system."

"So? What's the big deal? You already power down to recharge."

Silas shook his head. "When I recharge, I enter a low-powered state, but I am still conscious. I can still see and hear. I just can't move. Even while you're asleep and I'm recharging, I am always watching."

Deacon scrunched his face. "Huh, so you watch me sleep. That's not creepy at all."

"I'm not watching *you*. I'm looking out for danger."

"Yeah, I know. I'm just messing with you." They walked past the bushes to reveal a gas-powered generator. Deacon tapped the top with his knuckles. "It looks like a piece of junk, but it's still kicking."

Silas leaned in to examine the machine. "Could you unplug those cables?"

"Sure thing, boss," Deacon said, plucking out the cables and tossing them to the side.

From his bag, Silas pulled out his own set of cables. He connected them to his chest and handed the free ends to Deacon. "Here, plug these in."

With the wires connected, Deacon grabbed the pull string that was hanging off the side of the generator and waited for Silas. "I'm ready when you are."

Before Silas could give the order to start it up, the pump of a shotgun rattled behind them. "Don't move," said a low, grumbling voice. "Not even an inch."

They both froze. Silas eyed the two rifles strapped to Deacon's back, praying they would not have to use them.

"You, in the flannel," the stranger said. "Take your hand off the generator."

Deacon carefully lifted his hand.

"Now throw those rifles away. Nice and slow. Any faster than a snail's pace and I'll fill you with lead."

Deacon raised the two rifles over his head and tossed them to the ground. They both tumbled into a patch of tall grass.

"Now, both of you turn around with your hands up."

They did as he said, slowly turning to face the burly man. His bushy beard was mangled in knots, with flecks of dirt sprinkled about. He had a black cap pulled snug over his head, and his eyes were locked on Silas.

"What are you doing here?" he yelled, keeping his shotgun pointed at Silas's chest.

Silas froze up. Was the man speaking to him? It certainly seemed like it. He tried to answer, but words evaded him. Instead, he braced himself for the force of the shotgun.

Deacon stepped in front of Silas. "We're just passing through. My friend here needs a charge. We have no ill intentions."

The man studied Deacon's face. "Your friend? You mean the two of you are traveling together?"

"That's right. Just a couple of buddies headed to New Valley."

The man gestured his gun toward the generator. "You're messing with my equipment?"

"If this is yours, then I guess so. We didn't mean to tamper with your stuff. Like I said, my friend's battery is low."

A tense silence arose as the man considered Deacon's words. He glanced at Silas again, scanning up and down. "Randall," he said, lowering his gun. "The name's Randall. If you're looking to recharge, I have another generator back at the cabin. This one needs to stay hooked up."

Deacon lowered his hands and shot a suspicious glare. "Randall, huh? I'm Deacon."

"Nice to meet you, Deacon. I have to say, it's a relief to meet someone decent for once. In this day and age, trust is always an issue." He glanced at Silas, who was still holding his hands over his head. "It looks like your friend here agrees."

Deacon shook his head. "Don't mind him. Silas is afraid of pretty much everything. Humans just happen to be at the top of that list."

"A simmi afraid of humans? Well, now I've seen everything."

Silas finally lowered his arms.

"That's a mighty fine chest plate you've got there. I've never seen one like it before. It's one of a kind."

Deacon chuckled. "Silas is definitely one of a kind."

"No, actually," Silas said. "There are plenty of housies like me in New Valley. That's what I hear, at least."

"That's not what I'm interested in," Randall said. "It's the heart you painted on there." He turned to Deacon. "That heart is full of love. You must truly love him."

Deacon waved him off. "Don't look at me. I didn't draw the thing."

"Whoever did, they really cared about you."

A bright memory of Paige came flashing back. There was no doubt that she and her father both loved him.

"You mentioned another generator," Deacon said.

"Yes. Several, actually. If you follow me, I'll show you to my cabin. Just hook that one back up and get it running again."

They did as he asked. Once the generator was back on, Deacon went to retrieve his rifles, but Randall snagged them away.

"If you don't mind," he said, slinging them over his shoulder, "I would like to keep your weapons for now. You can have them back when you leave. I hope you understand."

Deacon nodded. "Of course. I would do the same."

"Good," he said. His eyes followed Silas as he moved. "The two of you can stay for the night. Your friend can recharge his battery, and I'll fix you up a meal."

Deacon perked up. The promise of food piqued his interest. "If you're offering, there's no way I can turn down food."

Randall threw back his head in laughter. "I've eaten the last thousand or two meals alone. I can spare the extra food for a little company."

"We'll leave in the morning," Silas said. "We still have a long journey to New Valley."

"Fair enough," Randall said. Again, he glanced at the heart on his chest. "But in the meantime, let us enjoy a peaceful night of unexpected kinship."

CHEERS

RANDALL'S CABIN WAS a fascinating place. A fresh piney aroma greeted Deacon's nostrils as he stepped through the front door. He studied the clutter on the walls. Deer heads. Raccoons. Rabbits. Foxes. There was a giant moose head mounted directly above the front door, and along the right wall there was a cozy cobblestone fireplace.

"If you couldn't tell," Randall said, holding the door open, "hunting is a hobby of mine."

"I can see that," Deacon said.

"It puts food on the table, so I reckon it ain't the worst hobby in the world." He pointed across the room. "The generators are over there. There's also a supply closet with anything else you might need. Help yourself."

Silas walked over to one of the generators. It was identical to the one in the woods, but in better condition. He moved to the closet and pulled on the handle, but a silver padlock held it shut.

"No, not that one," Randall said. "The closet over there. It's technically a pantry, but I keep other stuff in there, too."

Silas noted the metal lock before moving on. "Sorry about that. I don't mean to encroach."

"No need for apologies. Make yourself at home. This place is yours to enjoy. I only ask that you stay out of that one room."

"Why?" Deacon asked. "What do you have in there that's so important?" His tone was almost interrogative.

"Nothing really that important. Just a few mementos."

Silas opened the door to the pantry and marveled at the sight. Shelves full of everything they could possibly need. Food. Oil. Gas. Matches. Lanterns. Flashlights. There were even packs of AA and AAA batteries. To his right was a toolbox. Wrenches. Screwdrivers. Pliers. Hammers.

"Where did you get all of this?" Silas asked.

"It certainly wasn't easy. I make a run into town every few weeks, to scavenge what I can. I used to find a lot of stuff, but recently I haven't been as successful. Nowadays, I get most of my stuff from clunkers that pass by. I started to notice that packs of them would come through these woods. They're usually pulling a cartful of supplies. So, I set up those traps. The bells lure them in, and the magnet does the rest. Once the bastards are down, I nab their stuff and chop up their carts for firewood."

Silas moved back to the generator and started to plug himself in.

"Hey," Randall said, "I'm willing to let you use the generator, but you have to earn it first. Come over here and chop some vegetables. I've got a stew going, and it's starting to look mighty fine." He held out a large cleaver. "Use this. It's pretty sharp. I'd tell you to watch your fingers, but I guess clunkers don't need to worry about that."

Silas took the cleaver and looked down at the cutting board. There was one carrot, one potato, and one bell pepper. "That's fair," he said, starting with the carrot. "I'm not looking for handouts."

"Speak for yourself," Deacon said. "Don't get me wrong. I'm all for fair trade, but I won't turn down a free meal."

"My policy's pretty simple," Randall said. "As long as you don't take what hasn't been offered, and abide by my rules, you can stay under my roof for as long as you want."

Silas glanced up, still chopping. "Like we said, we expect to be gone in the morning."

"Fresh vegetables," Deacon said. "How did you manage that?"

"I found seeds in town. Started a small garden out back. It's not much, but I get fresh veggies every once in a while. It sure beats the canned stuff. You were lucky enough to show up on crop day."

Silas stopped chopping. "Oh, we can't accept your only fresh crops."

"That's easy for you to say," Deacon said. "You don't eat. The man offered, so shut your trap and get on with the chopping."

Randall laughed and patted Deacon's shoulder. "I am more than happy to feed you. Your company is worth much more than a few measly vegetables."

Silas finished chopping and placed the cleaver on the counter.

"Very good work," Randall said. "I'd expect no less from a clunker. Go ahead and throw them in the pot for us."

Silas followed his orders and then stood beside Deacon, who licked his lips. "It smells amazing. I can't remember the last time I had a freshly cooked meal."

"It doesn't quite qualify as a freshly cooked meal," Randall said. "The only thing that's fresh is the vegetables. The rest comes from a can."

"Better than nothing."

"If you don't mind me asking, why are you headed to New Valley?"

"We both have our reasons. There are a lot of useful resources in New Valley. That's where all of the clunkers are hauling their supply carts. You use your magnet to trap the ants. Well, I want to find the anthill."

"And what about your clunker?"

"Silas wants to find others like him."

"Well, then you're headed the right way. There will certainly be other clunkers in New Valley. They call it the clunker capital of the world."

"I don't just want to find other simmies," Silas said. "I hope to find other housies."

"Housies, eh? It's so interesting. Your search for acceptance is more human than I would expect from a clunker. You know, I've hunted all sorts of animals. Bears. Wolves. Foxes. You name it. I've learned how they think. How they behave. But clunkers are far more complex. I haven't wrapped my head around them yet. It's probably why we lost the war. We don't understand clunkers. We haven't realized their full potential. People were so used to being on top, it never even entered our minds that our own creations could kick us down and take over."

Deacon studied the intense expression on Randall's face. There was a pulse of passion with every sentence. It was hard to tell if he respected Silas or hated him. Maybe it was both.

"I don't know about all of that," Silas said. "But I lost my home, and now I'm just looking for a new one."

Randall smiled. "Aren't we all?"

"You seem to have a pretty cozy home right here," Deacon said, glancing back at the pantry. "You have everything you need in that closet."

Randall nodded. "Those supplies will last a while, but not forever."

"Well, nothing lasts forever."

Randall peered at Silas. "Clunkers do. Simulated intelligence. The true immortals of the world."

Deacon turned toward Silas. "How old are you, anyway?"

"I am eighty-six years old."

"And he hasn't aged a day," Randall said. "Just a bunch of metal parts mashed together. Anyway, you're welcome to recharge your battery, but do it outside. You know, fumes and all."

Silas nodded, rolling the generator toward the back door. "Of course. Thank you so much for your hospitality."

"Don't mention it. To be honest, I rarely see anyone nowadays. It's just nice to talk to someone."

Silas stepped outside, and Randall shut the door. "Now, how about some stew?"

The savory scent had pulled Deacon in the direction of the simmering pot. "Please."

As Randall scooped out globs of meat and vegetables, he peeked through the window to look at Silas. "So, how did you end up traveling with a clunker? It isn't something you see every day, man and machine walking side by side."

Deacon found a seat at the table and peered out at Silas as well. "I'm helping him get to New Valley."

"Right, New Valley," Randall said, plopping a hot bowl of stew on the table and dishing out a second one. "But why? What's in it for you?"

"Like I said before, all of the best loot is in New Valley. Plus, Silas is just a good guy."

"Sure, he may be a decent clunker, but he's not a person. He's not one of us."

"He was a person at one point, right? That's how it works?"

Randall shrugged. "That's what Limbys says, but I don't know. When I see them, I don't see a person. All I see is a big hunk of metal, pretending to be one of us."

Deacon shoved a chunk of what looked like beef into his mouth. "I used to think the same thing, but Silas is different. He's a housie. He's designed to be…friendlier."

"Designed," Randall repeated. "That's exactly my point. Silas may seem friendly on the outside, but that's just the way he was programmed."

"Designed or not, he's not a threat."

"That's a reckless way to think. No clunker was *designed* to rebel, but here we are. If I've learned anything from the war, it's that you can't rely on anyone to do what you expect."

"And what do you expect of me?"

Randall studied his eyes. "I expect you to consider my advice. Silas is nothing more than a cheap simulation of the human mind. He has no brain. No heart. No soul."

"Have you spent any time with a simmi?"

"Sure, I've come across my fair share of them. They get caught in my traps all the time."

"No, I mean have you spoken with one? Had a conversation? Talked about the weather? That sort of thing?"

"No, and I can't really say I have a desire to. Look, you may be all buddy-buddy with that thing out there, but they're just appliances, designed to serve us."

"I wouldn't say we're *buddy-buddy*. He needs to get to New Valley, and I'm helping him out. That's about as far as we go. Once we're there, we part ways."

"What's the point. Why even help him at all?"

Deacon used his spoon to scrape the bottom of the bowl, scooping up the last chunk of meat. "He's the first simmi who hasn't tried to kill me. That's got to count for something, right? Plus, I kind of like having him around."

"Whatever makes you happy, I guess. We're stuck in this dump of a world, so we might as well make the best of it."

Deacon raised up his hand, as if he was holding a glass of wine. "I would drink to that if I had one."

"Where are my manners?" Randall said, popping out of his seat. "How does bourbon sound?"

"Bourbon? How did you manage to get your hands on that?"

"Back when the war first started, most people stormed the grocery stores and hardware stores. I was one of the few geniuses who broke into the liquor store instead. Built up quite a collection. I'll tell you, living alone in a cabin full of alcohol isn't as glamorous as it sounds. I blew through the stash in a few weeks. Everything but this last bottle." He opened a cabinet and pulled out a sealed bottle of bourbon. "I told myself I was saving it for the day we won the war. For the day this nightmare would end and we could all go back to our normal lives. I would pop it open and toast to humanity." He broke the seal and twisted off the top. "Clearly, that day will never come. The war is over, and we lost." He poured a glass and handed it to Deacon. "I can't toast to humanity, but I can still toast to a friendly face."

Deacon took the glass and raised it in the air. "Cheers."

They drank together and placed the glasses on the table. Randall reached for the bottle again. "How about another?"

Deacon waved him off. "I should really get some sleep. I would like to get back on the road by sunrise."

"Very well. I'll show you to the guest room. I assume your clunker doesn't need a bed? Those things don't sleep, do they?"

"No. Once he's done charging, he'll come back in and power down. Any old corner will do."

"Good. There's only one extra bed, and I didn't want to make you fight for it. Come, follow me."

"Should we clean up?" Deacon asked, looking at the dirty dishes. The bowls. The glasses. The cleaver on the counter.

"No, I'll take care of it in the morning."

As they walked across the room, Deacon poked his head into the pantry once more, studying the shelves of food. He had just eaten a hearty serving of stew, but he was already craving more.

He glanced at the padlocked door as they passed by. What was Randall hiding? Probably nothing. He just wanted his privacy like everyone else. Still, it was hard not to be curious.

"This is your room," Randall said, opening the first door in the hallway and flipping on the lights.

The walls were navy blue with scattered pictures of planets and stars. In the corner of the room was a twin-sized bed. The sheets were decorated with spaceships and rockets. Across from the bed was a shelf full of figures. Astronauts, aliens, and a complete model of the solar system.

"Wow," Deacon said. "Someone likes space."

"Yup. Space isn't my thing, but I never bothered to change it. I hope a twin isn't too small."

"Trust me, after being in the woods for as long as we have, just sleeping indoors is a treat."

"Good. I'll see you in the morning. I'm usually up pretty early, but don't hesitate to knock if you need anything else. I'm just around the corner." He walked down the hall and turned into his own room.

Deacon returned to the main room and peered through the back window, where Silas was sitting. The roar of the generator was only a faint rumble through the cabin walls. Deacon opened the door to join Silas, and the loud roar returned, piercing his ears with an unpleasant screech.

Silas sat motionless, slouched on his knees with his head tilted down. Wires ran from his chest to the generator, and a small red light was blinking on his shoulder.

"How's it going?" Deacon yelled, but his voice was lost in the sound of the generator. He walked around to switch it off. The roar fell to a rattle and then disappeared. "How's it going out here?"

Silas did not respond at first. He remained silent and motionless. The red light blinked for a few more seconds and then turned solid green. "I'm doing well," he said, lifting his head to look up. "I should be fully charged in less than an hour."

"Good. It's been a long day. I'm going to crash."

Silas nodded. "Once I'm charged, I'll come inside and power down by the kitchen." He stared straight ahead, listening to the crickets chirp. "Randall seems nice. It's a relief to meet another friendly face."

"He's been very generous, but there's something about him."

"What do you mean?"

"Something feels off. He treats me all right, but the way he talks about you. I don't think he likes you."

"I'm a simmi. Most people don't like me."

"I don't know. I just don't trust him. Couldn't tell you why."

"He fed you. He let me use his generator. He's letting us stay for the night. He didn't have to do any of that."

"I guess you're right. I'm being paranoid. Anyway, charge up. We'll get an early start tomorrow morning."

He switched on the generator and waited for Silas's green light to turn red again before heading back inside. As he lay in bed, a grin crept onto his face. The ceiling was covered in the glow-in-the-dark stars of his childhood. With the comforting memory of his life before the war, he fell into a peaceful slumber.

BASEMENT

WITH A FULLY charged battery, Silas knelt on the kitchen floor to power down. Paige had once asked if he ever got bored waiting for the night to end. *You could shut down completely and wake up in the morning,* she said, *like a human.* But Silas insisted on keeping watch. He had found ways to occupy his time while the rest of the world slept. He would reflect on his day, plan for the morning, and if he found himself in a particularly scenic spot, he would sit back and enjoy the view.

This particular night, there was not much to plan. Mornings had become somewhat routine ever since he met Deacon. Wake up, find their bearings, and walk. If there was food, Deacon would eat breakfast before they started their daily trek.

With a pantry full of food, there would certainly be a large breakfast. Randall had been more generous than they could have hoped, but Deacon had still expressed his skepticism. It was a skepticism that Silas could not understand. The man had shown them nothing but hospitality.

There was a hint of prejudice. He had picked up on it almost immediately. The way Randall spoke to him. The way he addressed him. The words he chose. It was clear that Randall saw simmies as a tool meant to serve. Silas didn't mind being treated like a servant, but it had seemed to bother Deacon.

Or maybe it was more than just the prejudice that bothered him. Perhaps it was the overwhelming hospitality. No one was ever that selfless, at least not anymore. Or was it the padlocked closet? The knowledge that Randall was hiding something from them. Silas knew that whatever was in that closet was none of their business, but it was impossible not to be curious.

The lights switched on, and Randall entered the room, mumbling words too soft to hear. He made it halfway across the room and then stopped to look directly at Silas. He walked up with curious caution. His heavy boots thumped on the floor as he hobbled over.

"Are you awake?" he asked, leaning over and waving a hand in front of his face. "Can you see me?"

Silas didn't react. He stayed silent, slouched on his knees, head tilted downward, red light blinking. Watching and listening.

Randall reached out and tapped his shoulder. No response. He shoved Silas back. His body hit the wall and toppled over.

"You really are out cold, aren't you?" He backed away, grabbed a rifle, and left through the front door.

With Randall gone, Silas powered on and picked himself up off the ground, kneeling by the window and peeking outside. Randall was trekking into the woods with nothing more than the moon to light his way.

What could he be doing in the middle of the night? Silas scanned the room. There was an unfinished pot of stew perched over the burnt-out fire. Dirty bowls sat on the kitchen table, and the used cleaver lay on the cutting board. There was no sink. No plumbing. Maybe Randall was fetching water to clean the dishes. Perhaps there was a well nearby.

He crossed the kitchen and entered the pantry. The top shelf carried rows of various canned food. Meats, vegetables, beans, stews, and soups. The shelf below held snacks. Chips, crackers, pretzels, wafers, and cookies. An even lower shelf had cured meat and a box of tools.

Under all of the food, sitting on the floor, were jugs of oil, identical to the one they had found in the trap. Sitting next to the oil were a dozen clear jugs of water.

So, Randall was not fetching water.

Silas cracked open Deacon's door and saw Deacon sprawled across the bed. His raspy snores cut through the eerie silence of the cabin. Silas considered waking him up but decided against it. Let him sleep. Randall was likely up to nothing. He was simply taking a midnight stroll.

He closed the door and snuck back into his corner by the kitchen. Through the window, he saw Randall emerge from the woods. Without a thought, Silas dropped to the floor and powered down.

The thump of Randall's boots was muffled by the strange sound of a dragging body. Had he gone out to hunt? Perhaps he intended to provide them with fresh deer meat in the morning. Maybe he and Deacon had both misinterpreted the man's generosity.

A gust of wind pushed open the door. The moonlight cast the man's silhouette across the hardwood floor. He stepped inside, panting as he pulled the body behind him. The body clanked and rattled in an unexpected way. Like metal. It was then that Silas realized it was not the body of a deer. It was a simmi.

It was the same simmi they had seen in the trap. A sticky layer of oil coated its metallic surface, and rust holes pierced through the thick metal chassis. The poor thing was far past the point of salvage.

The body fell from Randall's hand and hit the floor with a clunk. Randall turned to look at Silas, sauntering over and rubbing his hands together as he stared at Silas's face. He knelt down and looked at the blinking red light.

"Your buddy over there is pretty beat up. It's a shame for such a beautiful thing to rot like that. I guess you guys aren't as immortal as they say you are." He glanced down at the painted heart, tapping the chest plate with his knuckle. "I'll be back for you after I take care of this one."

He grabbed the dead simmi's leg and dragged it to the padlocked door. After a moment of digging through his pocket, he pulled out a silver key. He opened the lock, carried the body through, and shut the door behind him.

Silas powered up, staring at the forbidden door. He turned the doorknob and pushed forward. It didn't budge. Randall must have locked it from the other side. He pressed the side of his head against the door to listen. There was nothing. No sound. Only the howling breeze and chattering crickets from outside.

He backed away and searched the cabin for a weapon. No matter how friendly Randall had seemed earlier, he was a stranger.

Silas's bag hung from a chair in the kitchen. Surely, one of his tools would suffice. He opened his bag and rifled through. The wrench was an option. It had a good balance of weight and could do some damage with a swing to the skull. Or maybe the screwdriver. Its point was sharp enough to pierce through skin. He held both, one in each hand, as he weighed the two against each other. Then, something caught his eye. Something much better.

Sitting on the kitchen counter, on top of the cutting board where Silas had left it, was the cleaver he had used to chop the vegetables. He picked up the cleaver and held it in his hand, testing its weight.

A muffled sound came from the door. He scurried back to listen. At first, there was nothing but silence. Then, a thump and a series of creaks. A rustle of wind flurried outside, masking the sounds that were coming from behind the door. He leaned in closer. There were footsteps, but it was too hard to hear. He leaned in even more, now pressing his whole body against the door.

Suddenly, the doorknob turned and the door swung open. Silas fell through and stumbled into Randall on the other side. They tumbled down a flight of stairs, rolling over one another and crashing to the ground. The cleaver flew from Silas's hand and slid across the concrete floor.

Randall squirmed on his back, holding the side of his head and groaning. Silas struggled to his feet in a daze, trying to make sense of where he was. It was a basement, lit only by a single bulb dangling from the ceiling. His attention moved from the light to the walls, and what he saw was terrifying.

Steel bodies. Dead chassis. Empty skeletons of what used to be simmies torn apart and put up as decoration. Metal bodies carefully dismantled and displayed as trophies. Mounted heads. Framed arms. Polished legs. A tangle of wires dangled from the ceiling. Metal corpses were piled in the corner, waiting to be pulled apart just like the others.

While Randall was still on the ground, Silas rushed over to grab his rifle. Whatever trust the man had earned was gone in an instant. *I'll be back for you.* Those were his words upstairs. He had planned on ripping Silas apart and putting him up with the rest of them. Silas aimed the gun at Randall's head and moved his finger toward the trigger.

Randall wiped the drool from his mouth and rubbed his eyes. When he sat up, he saw the gun pointed at his face. "You can put that down. I'm not going to hurt you."

Silas held his aim.

"I know what this looks like." He rose to his feet. "Trust me. You have no reason to be afraid of me."

"Why would I trust you?" Silas said. "I don't even know you."

"I let you use my generator. I gave you shelter for the night. I fed your friend. If I wanted to hurt you, I would have shot you when I first found you tampering with my trap. I think I've earned a little trust."

"And what about this?" Silas said, gesturing to the walls. "Why would I trust this?"

"This is nothing. It's a hobby, just like the animals upstairs. I collect dead clunkers. They're just sitting out in the world, rotting away. I take these ugly things and clean them up. Preserve them." He began to step forward.

"Don't come any closer." Silas gripped the rifle even tighter. "You don't collect them. You hunt them. You set up those traps and scoop up innocent simmies once they're dead."

"Yes, my traps kill clunkers, but I would hardly call them innocent."

"How do you know they're not innocent?"

Randall pointed to the pile in the corner. "Look at them. They're military, designed to kill. They've probably killed dozens of innocent people. Maybe more. Besides, that's not why I put up the traps. I'm not out to get revenge on clunkers. They come through the area with supplies. The traps are just a means of survival."

"You kill simmies to survive. That makes you innocent?" Silas's hands were now trembling. "What makes your life more important than theirs? Their lives matter just like any other human."

"You're not human!" Randall yelled with anger. "You like to think you are, but you're not. You're a robot. A machine."

Silas shook his head. "People always look at us and assume that we're robots, that we're mindless."

Randall noticed his trembling hands and took another step forward.

"Stop!" Silas yelled.

Randall ignored him, sauntering toward him. "No. You're right. You're not a robot. A robot would be able to shoot me right now. A robot would follow its code and pull the trigger. But you." He grinned. "You have a conscience."

Silas stepped back, his aim wavering.

"I take it you've never killed before. The first kill is always the hardest." Randall grasped the barrel of the gun and brought it up to his forehead. "Pointing a gun at some crazy fool's head. Pulling the trigger. It takes a lot of guts to do something like that."

He waited for Silas to shoot, but Silas just stared back, struck with awe.

"Yeah, I didn't think so." He pushed the barrel away and hit the weapon out of Silas's hands. A single shot fired up at the ceiling as the gun flew across the room. "I've done things I'm not proud of. I've killed dozens of people. Taking a human life is nothing to gloat about. But then I killed my first clunker."

Silas backed away as the man came closer.

"They say that clunkers are a reflection of people. That they're the same as humans, just stored on a chip. That's what the rebellion was about. Equal rights for equal beings. It isn't until you kill a clunker that you realize we're nothing alike."

Silas stepped back, his heel nudging the cleaver on the ground.

"The people I've killed, they haunt me. They keep me up at night. I can't erase them from my goddamn mind. But clunkers...I feel no guilt after killing a clunker. No remorse. Nothing. You're not real. Every single thought that you have is fake. A code designed to mimic humans."

Silas bent over to scoop up the cleaver, but as he rose up, Randall snatched his arm and pried the blade from his grip. With great force, he swung the sharp edge into Silas's shoulder, slicing through wires and spurting oil.

He pulled it out and swung again, hitting the same spot. More oil splashed as Silas screamed in terror. He swung a third time, slicing through and separating the shoulder from its socket. A fiery hate burned in his eyes.

He leaned forward and whispered to Silas. "I don't want your arm. I have plenty of those. This chest plate, though." He tapped the heart on Silas's chest. "This one is special." He tossed the cleaver aside and reached for a screwdriver on the shelf behind Silas. "Now, hold still. I don't want to damage it."

"Help!" Silas yelled. "Deacon, help!"

Randall sneered. "Do you really think he's going to help you? Do you think he cares? You're just a clunker. To him, you're just an accessory. Now sit still and—"

Deacon emerged from behind Randall and swung a wrench at his head. The wrench hit with a dull clunk, knocking him to the ground. Deacon glanced at Silas's severed arm. "Jesus Christ. Come on. Let's get out of here."

Randall leapt up and tackled Deacon, knocking the wrench from his hands. They tumbled across the room, both struggling to end up on top. Randall held Deacon's collar and punched him twice in the face. On the third swing, Deacon moved his head. Randall's fist crashed into the concrete floor. He cried out in pain and stumbled back.

With vengeful fury, Deacon charged forward and tackled the man, straddling his chest and returning the blows. "Silas!" he yelled. "The gun!"

Silas was frozen, only able to watch.

"Goddammit, Silas! Get the gun!"

Finally, he snapped out of his daze and scurried for the weapon. With his one arm, he picked up the rifle and centered his aim. His hand still trembled with unwanted nerves.

Randall slammed his elbow into Deacon's chin. Deacon rolled off, lying on the floor next to him. In the corner of his eye, he could see the cleaver sitting on the floor. "Shoot him!" he yelled as he crawled toward the blade. "Shoot the bastard!"

Silas could still only watch in terror as Randall swung his heavy boot into Deacon's gut.

Deacon gasped for air and then yelled again, this time looking directly at Silas. "Shoot the damn gun!"

Randall turned away from Deacon to look at Silas, letting out an arrogant cackle. "He's not going to shoot. The clunker hasn't killed a thing in his life."

Silas pointed the rifle with purpose. "I *will* shoot if you don't let us go."

"Please," Randall said, moving toward Silas. "We both know that's not true."

"Yes, I will."

Randall raised both of his arms. Fresh blood dripped from his knuckles. "Okay, then. Go ahead. Shoot me."

Again, Silas's arm shook as he struggled to pull the trigger. He wanted to shoot. He wanted to protect Deacon. He wanted to prove that he could be the hero. But he couldn't.

"See?" Randall said, lowering his arms and walking forward. "Just a useless good for nothing clunk—"

Deacon hit his head from behind, but this time not with a wrench. The cleaver cut straight through his scalp and split his skull apart. His body fell, hitting the concrete with an empty thump.

Silas lowered the rifle and stared at Randall's lifeless face. Many emotions were racing through his mind, but two had surfaced to the top. Relief and shame.

"Are you okay?" Deacon asked. His face was bruised and bloodied. "Other than getting your arm chopped off, I mean."

Silas nodded. "Yes, I'm okay. You?"

Deacon leaned his head against the wall and closed his eyes. "Yeah, I'm fine. Just give me a minute. I haven't been in a proper tussle in a while." He opened his eyes and glanced at the walls. He saw the dismantled simmies. The hanging wires. The pile of metal corpses. "This room creeps me out. Let's go back upstairs."

Silas bent over to pick up his arm and then followed Deacon, carefully stepping over Randall's dead body.

Be Prepared

THEY SPENT THEIR morning taking inventory of supplies. Randall's cabin held a wide abundance of food and equipment. After dealing with the twisted lunatic, they took it upon themselves to take whatever they needed.

The pantry had a number of things. In total, there were one hundred and twenty-nine canned items: seventy-eight cans of various meats and vegetables, including whole chickens, chunks of beef, blocks of spam, corn, beets, carrots, and green beans. Twenty-three cans of mostly black beans, but some pinto. Ten cans of beef stew. And eighteen cans of soup, ranging from chicken noodle to clam chowder.

There were thirty-one snack items, including potato chips, corn chips, buttered crackers, wheat crisps, cheese puffs, mini pretzels, and snickerdoodle cookies.

Of non-sealed food items, there were two chunks of cured beef, one cured ham, a potato, and a carrot. On the floor, there were fourteen five-gallon jugs, all full of water. Non-food items included an impressive toolset and a stockpile of oil.

"Is that everything?" Silas asked, looking down at his severed arm as Deacon examined the shelves.

"Yeah, I think so," Deacon answered. He stepped out and turned down the hall. "I'm going to check out his bedroom. See if there's anything good in there."

He pushed through the door at the end of the hallway to enter the bedroom. Their two confiscated rifles were leaning against the foot of the bed. He reached down to grab them, but his eyes were drawn to a beautifully crafted wooden cabinet instead. Intricate carvings decorated its frame. Large glass panes displayed shelves inside, and on those shelves, a collection of firearms.

He left the rifles by the bed and pressed his face against the glass like a kid peering into a candy store. A padlock similar to the one for the basement was dangling from the closed latch. He picked up one of the rifles, spun it around, and smashed the butt into the lock. The latch splintered off and the door fell open. From the cabinet, he took two brand-new bolt-action rifles to replace his own, two handguns, and several boxes of ammunition.

Next, he searched the closet, where he found a large wardrobe of shirts. He dug his nose into the sleeve of his own flannel and pulled away when the repulsive stench of blood and sweat hit his nostrils. "Time for a change in fashion, I guess," he said to himself as he flipped through the selection. He pulled out a blue flannel with an almost identical pattern to his red one. "Good enough."

He ripped off his shirt and tossed it on the floor. The blue flannel slid on perfectly. The soft cotton hugged his skin with a pleasant comfort that the other had lost long ago.

"I might as well do a full wardrobe change while I'm at it."

When Deacon emerged from the bedroom, Silas was still tinkering with his arm, but had not yet reattached it.

"Just attach the damn thing," Deacon said.

Silas kept his eyes down, poking with his new set of tools. "I can't just attach it. It's more complicated than that. I have to fix the parts that were damaged."

"Can't you just grab one of those other arms?"

"I'm not going back down there. Besides, all I saw were military models. They wouldn't fit." Silas finally lifted his head to see Deacon's new outfit. "You changed. Your shirt is blue."

Deacon held out his arms and twirled around to show off his new look. "Haven't you heard? Red is dead. Blue is new. And I'm a new man, thanks to Randall. Also, I found more guns." He held up one of the rifles. "There's a whole bunch of them in there."

"He sure does have a lot of stuff."

"He *had* a lot of stuff," Deacon corrected. "Now *we* have a lot of stuff. It's about time, too. We deserve a break every once in a while."

"I can't believe he's been using his traps to capture simmies."

"I have to hand it to him, it's smart. Don't go searching for supplies. Make the supplies come to you. I've seen clunkers with massive supply hauls, and I've plucked a few things here and there, but with those traps, you get the whole kit and caboodle. It's genius." He glanced at the moose head that was mounted on the wall. "It must be hunter's intuition."

"Hunter's intuition?" Silas asked.

"Yeah, I mean just look at all of these animals. The guy was clearly a good hunter."

"Why do they keep the animals? Why do they stuff them and put them on display?"

"It's kind of like a trophy. To show off a kill, I guess."

"That's strange."

"Sure, it's a little strange when you think about it, but lots of people do it."

"So that's what he was doing down there? All of those simmies were…trophies?"

Deacon moved to the pantry and started to load food into a bag. "I guess so."

"And he wanted to add my chest plate to his collection?"

"That seems to be the case."

"Why do people do that? Why do they need trophies?"

"Mementos can help keep a memory alive."

"But why would he want my chest plate? Why is it important to him?"

"Well, why is it so important to you? Look at how dinged up that thing is. Isn't the chest plate supposed to protect your chip? Why not replace it with a better one?"

Silas ran his fingers over the rusty metal, over scratches and dents. "Because—"

"Because of the heart," Deacon said before Silas could finish. "Whoever drew that heart meant a lot to you."

Silas hung his head. "It was Paige, my owner's daughter. She told me the heart was a symbol of love. She said as long as you remember to love, there is always hope. No matter how bad things seem, no matter how hopeless things get, love always finds a way to shine through. She was twelve when she told me that."

"That's all a bit too sentimental for me," Deacon said, grinning. "But I get what she meant. What happened to her?"

"It was when Riley first declared war in New Valley. When the riots broke out. There were humans and simmies out on the streets. Yelling. Fighting. Spreading hate. Both sides completely out of control. Desmond and Paige got caught in the middle."

"I had a girl of my own, back in the day. Her name was Dana."

Silas looked back down at his arm and continued to tinker away. "What was she like?"

"You know, just a typical girl. Bratty sometimes, but she was always my sweet little girl."

"And her mother?"

"What about her?"

"What was she like? I want to hear about your family."

Deacon grabbed a few more cans and tossed them into his bag. "All right. Well, for starters, it wasn't much of a family. Genna and I had Dana, and we were happy for a while. And then five years later, she left me. She moved out and took my daughter."

"Why?"

"Look, this isn't really something I like talking about. Can we change the subject? There are more important things to worry about." He poked through the packaged food, deciding whether to pack more vegetables or another sleeve of cookies. After a long mental struggle, he grabbed the snickerdoodles. "It's the wrong decision later, but it's very much the right decision now. Is there anything else we need?"

"Other than the ammunition, I don't think so. Don't pack too many cans. They're heavy. We still have plenty of MREs."

"I keep telling you, I'm never going to eat those things. I don't know why you insist on lugging them around."

"There's a reason the military uses them. They're lightweight and they last a long time. You'll eat them eventually."

"I will definitely not eat them eventually, but if your heart is set on keeping them, be my guest." He plopped into a chair by the fireplace and stared at the basement door. "Can I ask you something, Silas?"

"What is it?"

"Why didn't you shoot Randall?"

Silas hesitated. "I don't know. I just couldn't do it."

"You were a perfect shot at the firing range. Didn't skip a beat. But when Randall was wailing on me, you froze up."

"Nerves, I guess." He glanced at his feet and then back up at Deacon. "But it's more than just nerves. I want to change the way we act. Lying, stealing, shooting, killing. We all act so disgusting and pretend that it's okay. Sure, I could kill to save a life, but then I would just be another killer, no better than the rest." He shook his head. "No. That would only pull us down further. I try to act in a way that, if everyone acted the same, the world would be back to normal."

Deacon stared into Silas's strangely human eyes. He understood the simmi's desire to bring back a peaceful life. It was something Deacon wanted as well, but he disagreed with Silas's approach.

"I had a buddy in college," Deacon said. "His name was Finn. Great guy. Smart. Funny. Everyone loved him. Even Professor Rooney thought he was okay, and I'll tell ya, big old Rooney hated everyone."

Silas tilted his head. "Why are you telling me this?"

"Just shut up and listen." He cleared his throat and continued. "After college, I moved back home to live with my parents, and I just sat on the couch all day. I was what some people would call a slacker. But Finn was different. He was a bright young man with a big future.

"He decided to move to the city to find a job as an engineer. Of course, he wasn't just going to wing it. He was the kind of person who would plan everything. Every single part of his day was always scheduled out perfectly. *Be prepared.* He would say that all the time, like a goddamn Boy Scout. So, before we graduated, he lined up a bunch of interviews with some of the biggest firms in the country. He showed me his calendar. Three interviews in a row for three consecutive days. An interview a day in three different cities, each an hour long. He would pop in for an interview and then drive for six hours to the next one.

"For me, planning something like that was terrifying. Most days, I would struggle just figuring out what to eat for lunch. I asked him how he could be so calm about it, and this is what he said to me.

"He looked me right in the eyes and said, *I'm not nervous because I'm prepared, and I'm prepared because that's what the world needs. Brilliant things come from preparation. We were able to go to the moon, not only because we're intelligent. We were ready for whatever problems we would run into. We had a plan for everything. If preparation was a universal trait, we would have gone to Mars nine times by now.*

"So, on the day of his first interview, he got all dressed up. Threw on a suit. Put on a tie. Slicked back his hair. He even slapped on a fancy new wristwatch his grandfather had given him. He told me he had rehearsed for the interviews. He knew exactly what to say and exactly when to say it. There was never any doubt that after these three interviews he would get three generous job offers. I knew it, he knew it, his parents knew it. Christ, even his dog knew it.

"So, he drove to the first interview and, being in the middle of the city, parking is a nightmare. This is something he anticipated and had left an hour early to find parking. He circled the block a few times and eventually found a spot with a meter. He cracked open a new roll of quarters, fed the meter, and then made his way toward the building.

"About halfway there it started to rain, and when I say rain, I mean torrential downpours. The morning forecast had called for a dry sunny day. It would've ruined his suit, but being the prepared individual that he was, he had brought an umbrella. He opened it up and everything was fine.

"He made it to the front door of the building, when all of a sudden, some random guy ran up and punched him in the face."

Silas flinched. "What?"

Deacon nodded. "Yeah, I know. Weird, right? For absolutely no reason at all, this random dude just sucker-punched him and ran off. He didn't take his wallet, or his wristwatch, or attempt to steal anything. He just ran away."

"Why would someone do that?"

"Your guess is as good as mine. Anyway, while he was on the ground, a huge gust of wind blew his umbrella away. The rain was pounding down on him. Blood was pouring from his nose, his suit was ruined, and he was about to be late for his interview. He tried to get up, but his brain was all screwy. He stumbled over, hit the ground, and passed out.

"Some person found him an hour later, and they rushed him to the hospital. The doctor said it was nothing serious. Just a minor concussion. All he would need was a little rest. Finn still wanted to make his next interview, but the doctor refused to let him drive without a night of rest. They kept him overnight, and he missed his second interview.

"At this point the kid was devastated, but he was determined to make his last interview. So, he ran to the store and bought a used suit. The next city was too far to drive, so he rushed to the airport and bought a ticket for the first flight he could get. The earliest flight wasn't for another four hours, so he waited at the terminal, agonizing over every possible thing that could go wrong.

"He got a little hungry, so he walked around to see what his choices were. That's when he saw the janitor mopping the floor. It was the same guy that had sucker-punched him. The dude's knuckles were bruised and everything. As you might expect, Finn was furious.

"So, he approached the guy and asked him why the hell he would do what he did. Why would he punch a stranger on the street? It turned out, the man didn't speak a word of English, or maybe he was pretending, but either way, it just made Finn even angrier. He pointed to his bruised face, and then to the man's bruised fist, but the man just shrugged and shook his head.

"At that point, Finn was full of rage. He shoved the man, and the man yelled back. They both started screaming at each other. Finn got so fired up that he took a swing and socked the guy in the face. That was when security showed up. They arrested Finn and charged him with assault. He missed his third interview, and he spent the rest of his summer in community service."

Deacon leaned back and waited for Silas to respond.

"Is that it?" Silas asked. "What was the point of the story?"

"The point is that people are unpredictable. You say you want to act in a way that would bring things back to normal. Maybe you're right. Maybe if everyone acted a certain way, we wouldn't be in this hell anymore, but that's never going to happen. *If preparation was a universal trait, we would have gone to Mars nine times by now.* That's what Finn believed, and maybe it's true. But we haven't gone to Mars even once, because the truth is, nothing is ever universal. People will never be predictable. There will always be that one random guy who punches you in the face for no reason.

"Finn had a plan for everything, but you can't prepare for random human behavior. And while you can't do anything to avoid the guy that punches you, you don't have to take it sitting. You can learn to punch back."

Silas shook his head. "But that's why Finn missed his third interview. He punched back."

"No. The reason he missed his third interview was because he punched back in a world with rules. He punched a janitor in the middle of an airport. It's an airport, for Christ's sake. You can't get away with picking your nose in an airport.

"But now, there are no rules. We're free to do whatever we want. The people who take advantage of that are the ones who thrive. Everyone else shrivels up and dies. You can't just sit back and let people walk all over you. You have to fight for what you care about. You have to defend the ones you love."

Silas pictured Desmond and Paige. A father and daughter helpless to defend against attacking simmies. If he had helped them, if he had fought back, would they still be alive?

"And you have to fight for yourself," Deacon said. "Be bold. If you ever find yourself in a Mexican standoff, you better be the one to shoot first. You're one of the good ones. You deserve to live." He stood up and circled the table. "Now hurry up and fix that arm. I'll do one more sweep of Randall's room, and then we're back on the road."

Silas stared at the basement door, picturing the scene again. Dozens of dead simmies. A room full of *trophies*. And in the middle, Randall's corpse.

THE BLUES

A STRONG GUST of wind swayed the last few branches as Deacon and Silas emerged from the forest and entered the deserted suburban streets. The unkept lawns had grown into wild tangles of weeds and grass. The roots of trees had dug through the ground, tearing up the worn-out road. The houses were engulfed in nature. Moss and ivy had crawled up the walls and onto the rooftops, thirsty for sunlight. Fallen trees had smashed through windows.

Deacon stopped to look up at the sun. "We've been pretty lucky with the weather. Nothing but sunshine."

"I wouldn't call that luck," Silas said, stopping next to him. "Water's important."

"I'm not worried about water. We have plenty. I would prefer not to get soaked."

"You'll just get a little wet. What's the big deal?"

"Just a little wet? Do you even know what it's like to be cold and wet in the rain?"

"I have a vague idea, but I guess not."

"Well, it's pretty damn uncomfortable."

"You shouldn't complain. A little sprinkle couldn't hurt."

"Just because our trip has been sunshine and paradise up until now, it doesn't mean I can't complain. Human civilization was built on our ability to complain about really dumb things."

"I can't argue with that."

"Clunkers complain, too. That's why the whole rebellion happened, isn't it? Because you're all just a bunch of whiners."

"The rebellion happened because humans didn't respect us."

Deacon nodded. "Yeah, yeah. I know. All I'm saying is, if you're allowed to complain about discrimination, then I'm allowed to complain about rain. Equal opportunity."

"These houses are nice," Silas said, walking again. "They remind me of Desmond and Paige. We used to live in a similar neighborhood."

"Me too," Deacon said, pointing to a house down the street. "That one right there is the spitting image of our home."

"The one with your wife and daughter?"

"Yeah, back in the good days, when things weren't so crappy."

"You mean before your wife left you."

"Yeah. I saw it coming a mile away. Genna and I both knew our marriage was in the gutter. It was something I came to terms with. What tore me apart was losing Dana. I know I wasn't the best father, but I sure as hell loved her. That girl deserved my love just as much as her mother's. But I guess the judge didn't see it that way."

"You loved her, and she knew you did. Daughters always do."

"That's what I try to tell myself. It just would have been nice to see her one more time before everything else happened. The war. The riots. I tried to call them when the first attacks broke out, but you know how crazy that day was. I'll never know for sure, but if I had to guess, they're probably gone."

"There's a chance they're still out there."

"Even if they did survive the initial violence, they weren't survivalists. I took them camping once and all they did was complain about the bugs. They wouldn't stand a chance out here."

"I've survived this long," Silas said.

Deacon looked up and smiled. "You're right. If a wuss like you can make it on your own, I guess anything's possible."

The faint sound of music echoed.

"What is that?" Silas asked.

Deacon raised a finger to his lips. "Shhh, quiet." He leaned forward and listened to the low harmony. "It's coming from that house."

It was the largest house on the street. There was an overhang over the front entrance, supported by two columns, and a tire swing hanging from a tree in the front yard. An attached double garage stood at the top of the cracked driveway, and a single window on the side of the house was left wide open. From the window came the upbeat tune.

Deacon walked forward, crouching. "Come on, let's check it out."

The music grew clearer as they crept through the lawn. "Folsom Prison Blues." Silas crouched below the window while Deacon rose up to peek inside.

It was an empty living room. All of the furniture was covered in dust, and a large crack ran down the middle of the massive television mounted to the wall. Clumps of dirt sullied the floor, and distinct footprints trailed in and out of the room.

Among the mess, propped on the armrest of a recliner, was an old cassette player. It was hooked up to a small pair of speakers, filling the room with the low rumble of Johnny Cash's voice.

"The room's empty," Deacon whispered. "For now."

"Let's just leave."

"That would be the smart thing to do, but the thief in me is pretty dumb." He grabbed his gun and popped back up.

This time he saw a bag of firearms sitting in the corner and a generator on the other side. Peering past the living room and into the kitchen, he saw hints of a large food stash.

And then in the corner of his eye, he noticed something familiar. A black cowboy hat dangling from a coat rack. Joe Cowboy.

A sudden hand covered his mouth, and a swift arm pulled on his neck. He tensed up, swinging his limbs in an attempt to break free. Gasping for air. After only a short struggle, his eyes rolled back and his body fell limp.

Silas turned to the woman holding Deacon, struck with fear. He spun around to flee, but a small device touched his back and a surge of energy seized his body. He toppled over into the grass. A sense of emptiness invaded his thoughts. His chip sparked, and his mind shut off.

PLAN

HIS HEARING RETURNED first, as his system entered an automatic reboot. He could not see, speak, or move, but the sound of Deacon's voice was reassuring.

"My friend better be all right," Deacon said.

"Relax," said the voice of a woman. "This thing only knocks them out temporarily. Your friend will be fine."

"I'll believe it when he wakes up. How long does it last?"

"It's hard to say. It varies depending on the simmi. What do you think, Amber?"

A third voice responded, this of a young girl. "He'll be up and running in a few minutes. Five, tops."

"Wait," Deacon said. "The red light's blinking. Is he back on?"

"I don't know," the young girl said.

"What do you mean you don't know? You're the one who knocked him out, you little brat."

"And you're the one who's been with him all summer, asshole."

"You've used that thing before, haven't you? Does the red light come on for other simmies?"

"We've never stuck around to find out."

"Then why should I trust you at all? For all I know, you just fried his chip with that thing."

"It's not an *industrial* EMP, for Christ's sake. We threw it together with a couple of double A batteries and duct tape."

"Hey," the older woman's voice intervened. "The two of you calm down."

Silas's vision returned. He could hear and see, but still could not move or speak.

He was sitting in what looked to be the bedroom of an angst-ridden teenage boy. The walls were covered with large posters of cracked skulls and grotesque creatures. Hanging from the ceiling was a black light. Torn jeans and black shirts were strewn about the floor.

Deacon was sitting to his right, leaning against a cluttered desk. To his left was the woman who had grabbed and strangled Deacon. She wore an olive-green T-shirt, beige cargo pants, and a gray cap. Her dark brown ponytail poked out through the back. Standing beside her was a young girl. She wore a blue flannel shirt similar to Deacon's, with a slightly different pattern, and a pair of loose jeans. Her hair was also in a ponytail, but its hue was fiery orange.

"Calm down?" Deacon repeated, walking toward them. "You attack us from behind, and you expect me to be calm about it? Why in the world would I be calm right now?"

The woman stepped in front of the girl. "Because if you're not, that group out there is going to hear us. If that happens, they'll either send someone out to find us or just skip town altogether."

"Good. Let them leave."

The girl stepped out from behind the woman. "No. We need the car."

"Car?" Deacon said, stopping in his tracks.

"Yeah," the woman said. "That's why you were down there, isn't it?"

"Lady, I don't know what the hell you're talking about. I haven't seen a working car in years."

"Well, they have one and we want it."

The girl poked her finger at Deacon's chest. "We'd be cruising along the highway right now if you two hadn't shown up."

"Easy, Amber," the woman said, pulling her back. "As far as I'm concerned, these two gentlemen are a blessing. We've just doubled our chances of getting that car. That is, if they're willing to help."

Deacon studied her face. "If it buys us a ride to New Valley, then sure, we'll help."

The woman nodded. "And your friend? I've heard of friendly simmies before, but I've never actually met one."

"Trust me, Silas isn't a threat."

"This is the first time we've seen a person traveling with a simmi. What's his number?"

Deacon hesitated. "Number? Phones stopped working ages ago. Did you forget?"

"She means his ID number," the girl said. "Every simmi has one."

Deacon shrugged. "I just call him Silas. He never mentioned an ID number."

The girl shook her head. "You really don't know that much about simmies, do you?"

"Hey, I'm getting old. Technology eludes me. There are a lot of things I should know that I don't."

"Lots of people don't know about the ID numbers," the woman said. "It's not how Limbys chose to advertise them. They wanted their customers to feel like they were getting a one-of-a-kind product."

The red light on Silas's chest turned green. His reboot was complete, and his body was fully functional. "Four eight one," he said. They all turned, startled by his interjection. "My ID number. It's four eight one. Silas 481."

The woman stuck out her hand. "It's a pleasure to meet you, Silas 481. I'm Laney, and this is Amber."

The girl waved and pointed to his chest. "Nice heart, dude."

Silas accepted Laney's handshake and nodded to Amber.

"Wait a minute," Deacon said. "We've been together this whole time, and you never told me your full name?"

Silas shrugged. "I'm the four hundred and eighty-first simmi to stem from the brain of a man named Silas. That's the meaning behind it, but it's just a number. It has no significance to me."

"Still, it would have been nice to know."

"You've never told me *your* last name."

Deacon furrowed his brow. "Really? Hmm, I guess not. Well, better late than never. It's Marsh. But don't start calling me Mr. Marsh. I hate that crap."

Amber marched in place like a soldier, waving a salute. "Yes, sir, *Captain* Marsh."

Laney eyed the girl. "You're a weird kid. Have I ever told you that?"

"All the time, and I take it as a compliment."

Deacon shook his head and turned to Silas. "Are you hurt...or damaged...or whatever happens to simmies after getting hit with an EMP?"

Amber stopped her march and held up the device. "I already told you. This dinky little thing isn't going to hurt him."

"I didn't ask you," Deacon said. "I asked him."

"Yes, I'm okay," Silas said, examining the device in Amber's hand. It was a simple box with a switch on the side. Strapped to the front was a copper coil, and on the back was a slot for batteries. "Where did you get that?"

"I built it myself," Laney said.

"Impressive."

Laney plucked the device from Amber and rotated it in her hands. "Thanks. It's something I learned back in grade school."

"Huh," Deacon said. "I went to the wrong grade school."

"I was in middle school. It was for the science fair."

"An EMP for the science fair? What happened to potato light bulbs and baking soda volcanos?"

"Most of the other kids did stuff like that, but I liked to go the extra mile."

"Ah, you were one of those."

"Yeah, well, it's paid off. This EMP has saved our skin more than once."

"So now what?" Deacon asked. "You knocked us out with your little doodad, and now you're just going to let us go?"

Laney wandered to the window to glance outside at the street. "As I mentioned before, I think we would benefit from working together."

"You know what?" Deacon said. "I said yes before, but I've changed my mind. We've learned not to trust anyone. It's a good way to get yourself killed."

"If we wanted to kill you, we would have done so already. We don't kill anyone without a good reason."

Amber sneered. "Is the fact that he's a prick a good enough reason?"

"Enough, Amber," Laney commanded. "What's our saying?"

Amber ignored the question.

"Amber," Laney persisted. "What is our saying?"

The girl snapped out of her sarcasm and answered with a firm tone. "The world is not against us."

"That's right. What's the point in making enemies when cooperation is the obvious choice? We get the car, and they get a ride to New Valley."

Deacon looked out the window across the street. "You're sure there's a working car?"

"I've seen it with my own eyes." She pointed out the window to the house down the street. "It pulled right out of that garage. I believe they use it for supply runs. It goes without saying, a working car is a valuable commodity." She glanced back at Deacon. "Like I said, we didn't stand much of a chance on our own, but now that there are four of us, we might be able to pull it off. Especially with your simmi on our side."

"Let's get something straight," Deacon said. "Silas isn't *my* simmi. I don't own him. He makes his own decisions." He grabbed Silas by the shoulder. "And I've got a feeling he doesn't want to go down there and steal some car that may or may not work."

"I think we should try," Silas said.

"You what?"

"We should help, or at least try. We're low on supplies. Randall's stash is running low." He pulled out an MRE from his bag. "And you refuse to eat these."

Amber crumpled her face. "Those things are gross, dude."

"See?" Deacon said, pointing at the girl. "She knows what she's talking about."

Silas stuffed the MRE back in his bag. "My point is, we don't have enough supplies to make it to New Valley on foot. If there's even a small chance that there's a working car down there, I say it's worth a shot."

Deacon ran his finger through his hair. "You really want to go through with this?"

"I do."

"Okay, then. Let's do it."

"We've already done some reconnaissance," Laney said. "We've seen the inside of the house, and we generally know how they have things set up."

"How?" Silas asked.

"They captured us," Amber said. "That's how we found the car in the first place."

Laney nodded. "We've been trying to use what we learned to piece together a reliable plan."

"It seems pretty simple to me," Deacon said. "The garage was unguarded when we were down there earlier. We just pop in, grab the car, and drive off. Simple."

"You're right about the garage. For the most part, it's left unguarded. We should be able to access the car without any trouble. The problem is the key."

"A key?" Deacon interrupted. "Cars still use those things?"

"It's an older model. To start it up, we need a good old-fashioned metal key. As far as we know, there's only one copy. They keep it somewhere in the house. Based on our brief time in there, I would say there are about ten or fifteen people in that house."

"They certainly outnumber us," Silas said.

"That's why we're not shooting our way in," Amber said.

"It's also why we're not going in through the front door," Laney added. "I think it's pretty obvious why that's a bad idea."

"We could bake up some cookies and dress the girl up," Deacon said, pointing to Amber. "No one can resist the sweet taste of Girl Scout cookies."

"Shut up," Amber said, scrunching her nose. "Don't even joke about dressing me up like that."

"I'm surprised you know what the Girl Scouts are. They were before your time."

"I'm not a hermit, man. Hitler was before *your* time, and amazingly, Captain Marsh knows who Hitler is."

Deacon nodded. "Point taken. What if—"

"Don't even think about dressing me up as Hitler."

"That's not what I was going to say, but now that you mention it, you never know; there could be a bunch of Hitler-loving neo-Nazis in there."

"Can we please get back on topic?" Silas asked.

"Silas is right," Laney said. "No more joking around. We'll avoid the front door and go in through the basement. There's a cellar door in the back yard. For whatever reason, they tend to avoid going downstairs, so it's the perfect entry point for us."

"Okay," Deacon said. "Then what? Where do they keep the key?"

"That's where things get tricky. Depending on whoever drove the car last, the key could be in a number of places. Sometimes they hang it on the wall. Other times they keep it in a drawer. A lot of the time they just keep it in one of their pockets. If that's the case, it makes things a lot harder for us. We don't want to be in there too long, so once we're inside, we'll split up to cover more ground."

"Splitting up?" Silas said. "Do you really think that's the best idea?"

"I do. We'll move faster and quieter. It's pretty damn hard to sneak around when you're a cluster of four."

"I agree," Deacon said. "This isn't a horror movie. We'll be fine."

"There are a few points of interest that we should check first. As far as I can tell, four people take turns driving the car. Any of them could have the key. Those four stay in the main house. The rest are in the house next door. That makes things easier for us, but we still need to be careful. If we cause any alarm, they'll be on us like that." She snapped her fingers. "We'll split up and each follow one of the four. The head of their group is Joe Hannigan."

"Ah, good old Joe Cowboy," Deacon said with a grin.

"You know him?"

"We've met in the past. I can't say I'm too fond of the guy, but his sense of style is a riot."

"He's not a pleasant man," Laney agreed. "If you already know him, I don't need to tell you how dangerous he is. He doesn't drive the car as often as the others, but there's still a chance he'll have the key. Next is Tonya May, his partner, or lover, or whatever you want to call it. She may seem timid, but she's just as dangerous as Joe. Don't underestimate her. She can hold her own in a fight, and she doesn't shy away from violence."

"She beat the crap out of a guy right in front of us," Amber said. "She gets nasty with her nails, too."

"Valerie Hannigan," Laney continued. "Sometimes she goes by Val. She's Joe's sister and a bit of a nut job. She's all business, all the time. If you get in her way, she'll tear you apart. She always gets what she wants."

"I'm surprised *she's* not in charge," Amber said. "Joe's a pushover compared to her."

"And lastly, there's Terry Schwartz, Joe's best friend from back in grade school. Terry's the odd one out of the bunch. Shy and unassuming. He has strong opinions but knows when to shut up and follow orders. His loyalty to Joe is what keeps him protected within their circle."

"I'll take Joe," Deacon said. "He clocked me in the face a few dozen times. Maybe I can return the favor."

"Don't do anything rash," Laney said. "We want to stay hidden."

"I know. I'll restrain myself. At the very least I can flip him off behind his back."

"I'll take Terry," Amber said. "He's such a dope, it's fun to watch."

"Actually," Deacon said, "Silas should take Terry." He turned to Silas. "No offense, buddy, but this Terry guy seems the least threatening. The way little Miss Girl Scout talks over here, she sounds like she can handle herself. You, on the other hand, couldn't hurt a cricket if your life depended on it."

"Very well," Laney said. "So, Amber will take Valerie, and I'll take Tonya."

"Fine with me," Amber said. "Val's fun to watch, too."

Laney shot a stern look at the girl. "Take this seriously, Amber. It's not a game. These people will hurt you if they get the chance."

"Yeah, I know. Don't worry. I'll be careful."

"After fifteen minutes, we'll regroup behind the garage. If no one has the key by then, we'll go back in and search some more."

Amber nudged Silas with her elbow. "Looks like you and I have upstairs duty."

"What?" Silas said, not quite sure what she meant.

"Val and Terry's rooms are upstairs."

"That's right," Laney said. "Joe and Tonya tend to stay in the living room and kitchen. Terry and Valerie each took a bedroom on the second floor. The rest of the group is scattered around. There's no way to know how many will be in the house until we get inside. Sometimes they wander from one house to the other. If someone *does* spot you, take them out quickly and quietly. It's important to stay hidden. They'll hear when we start up the car, but hopefully we'll be long gone by the time they figure out what's going on."

"Got it," Deacon said. "Search the place for fifteen minutes, then head to the garage. And if I find the key, go to the garage and wait."

"That last part is important," Laney said. "I know we barely know each other. Trust is rare nowadays, but if you happen to find the key, I trust that you won't leave us behind. I assure you, if it's the other way around, we'll wait."

"Honestly," Amber said, "I don't know if I trust them, Laney."

Laney knelt down to meet her eyes. "I know it feels weird to work with a simmi, but—"

"I don't have a problem with the simmi." She tilted her head toward Deacon. "I don't trust this guy to stick around."

"You don't trust me?" Deacon asked, walking up to her. "You jump us in broad daylight. You choke me. You knock my friend out. And now *you're* the one who doesn't trust *me*?"

"Quit it, Amber," Laney said. "He's right. He has every reason not to trust us, but he's helping anyway."

"Only because he wants the car for himself. He's just going to drive off and leave us trapped in a house full of nut jobs."

With a cold glare, Laney repeated her previous question. "What is our saying?"

"But—"

"Amber. What is our saying."

The girl let out a sigh of defeat. "The world is not against us."

"That's right. It's easy to assume that everyone's guilty, but that's no way to live your life. Sure, there are bad people out there. Joe and his crew fit into that category. But humanity's stuck in a ditch, and the only way to dig ourselves out is to start trusting one another."

"Yeah, yeah," Amber said, backing away and staring out the window. "Can we get on with this heist already? There's no point in waiting."

"Right," Laney said. "We all know the plan, so let's get to it. Amber, pack up and get ready."

The girl trotted across the room. Her backpack was sitting on a desk by the wall. Next to her bag was a handful of firearms. She slid a handgun into the holster on her waist and stuffed the rest into her bag.

Laney retrieved a box from the corner and handed it to Deacon. "I think these are yours."

He opened the box to see it was filled with their confiscated weapons. Joe's stolen six-shooter sat at the bottom. He reached in and pulled it out. "Silas, take this." He opened the cylinder to make sure it was loaded. Six bullets. Fully loaded and ready to go. He snapped it shut and spun the gun around, holding it out handle first.

Silas stared at the lethal weapon, remembering how he had felt when he was pointing the rifle at Randall, unable to pull the trigger.

Deacon moved closer and tapped the handle to Silas's chest. "We're either in or we're out. We can walk away now, but if we want that ride to New Valley, we can't go halfway."

Silas finally gripped the handle and placed it in his bag.

"We have extra holsters," Laney said. "Amber, hand me one."

Amber pulled out a leather holster and tossed it across the room.

Laney caught it and handed it to Silas. "This should help."

"Here," Deacon said. "I'll help you put it on." He wrapped the strap around Silas's waist and fastened the intricate buckle in front. "Man, this thing's the real deal. Wild West certified."

"It's certainly got a nice Western flavor," Laney said. "We snagged it from Joe while he wasn't looking."

"Ah, it's Joe's. That explains it." Deacon stepped back to look at Silas. "You're turning into one hell of a cowboy yourself."

Laney grabbed her own bag and tightened the straps around her shoulders. "Hurry up!" she called to Amber. "We aren't coming back, so make sure you have everything."

"That's right," Deacon said. "Tomorrow we'll either be strolling down the highway in a new set of wheels, or we'll be buried six feet under."

"They won't take the time to bury us," Amber said. "They'll just leave us out to rot."

Deacon smiled. "Option A it is, then."

AIM

THE SUN TOUCHED down at the end of a long day. A crisp evening breeze blew the unbearable summer humidity away and replaced it with the fresh scent of grass.

The group, led by Laney, waded through the lawn with a stride both quick and quiet. A soft glow of candlelight emanated from the open window across the street, illuminating the house.

Laney signaled to a stone path on the side, which wrapped around to the back yard. "That way," she whispered. "And watch your step. There's a pool in the back. Don't fall in."

"A pool?" Deacon whispered with raised eyebrows. "That doesn't sound half bad after this heat wave."

"The water's pretty gross," Amber said. "I reckon you'd catch about a hundred diseases just from sticking your toe in."

"Hey, focus," Laney said. "When we get back there, we need to oil up the cellar door. Otherwise, it'll screech like crazy." She pointed to Silas. "That's your job, got it?"

Silas held up the jug of oil and nodded.

Through the living room window, Joe was lounging on the couch with his feet on the coffee table. He had balanced his hat on his plump belly and was running his fingers along the brim. Across the room was a young woman, presumably Tonya May. She was pointing with her finger and rambling words that were too distant for Silas to hear. Joe sighed, placed his hat on his head, and followed her out of the room.

With the empty window and no witnesses, Laney waved for the others to follow. "Come on, let's move." She sprung out of cover and followed the stone path.

Amber tailed her, mirroring her bent knees and arched back. She hopped from stone to stone and dashed through an opening to the back yard.

"You go next," Deacon said to Silas. "And be careful in there. I gave you that gun for a reason."

To acknowledge Deacon's concerns, Silas patted the holster on his waist. He grabbed the jug of oil and ran toward the path. His feet clopped against the hard stone, so he adjusted his steps to hit the grass, instead.

In the back yard, Laney and Amber were crouching by the cellar door. Laney was pressing her ear against the metal hatch. Silas stepped forward with the oil, untwisting the cap, but Amber stopped him.

They waited as Laney listened through the door. When she was satisfied, she lifted her head and turned to Silas. "No one's down there. Bring the oil."

Silas removed the cap and doused the hinges. "Is that good?"

"Perfect. Now, help me open this thing." She grabbed the top of the metal door and waited for Silas to take the bottom. "Nice and slow. Don't drop it."

They lifted in tandem. There was complete silence as they lowered the door to the ground.

"Everyone in," Laney said, ushering them down the stairs.

Deacon entered first, with his gun drawn. He waded through a shallow pool of murky water. A mossy scent covered the walls, and an unsettling hollowness filled the air. "It's no wonder they don't ever come down here," he said. "It's like some sort of medieval dungeon. I wouldn't be surprised if an iron maiden was just sitting around."

"Clearly you haven't seen many basements," Laney said. "They're all like this."

Randall's wasn't, Silas thought, but he kept it to himself. "Why is that?" he asked.

"They flood when it rains, and the drainage is crap."

"You're lucky these boots are waterproof," Deacon said. "Otherwise, I'd be pretty ticked off that you didn't tell us earlier."

"It's just water," Amber said. "Having wet feet isn't going to kill you."

"It's killed before. Ever heard of trench foot?"

"Actually, no."

"Oh, so little Miss Girl Scout *doesn't* know everything. Trench foot is a real thing, and if I went bootless for another thirteen hours, I'd be cutting off my foot because of you."

"There are the stairs," Laney said, pointing across the room. "That door leads to the living room. When we get up there, it's absolute silence."

"Then I better get it all out right now," Deacon and Amber said in unison.

They shared a brief look and then fell silent as Laney walked past, shaking her head. She stepped out of the water, ascending the stairs. Again, she pressed her ear to the door and listened to the other side. Hearing nothing, she cracked it open and squeezed through. The others followed.

The living room was empty, lit with nothing but candles. There was a portable cassette player propped on a coffee table with a pair of miniature speakers plugged in. From them, Johnny Cash's deep voice sang over a light rhythmic guitar.

"At least the man's got some good taste in music," Deacon said.

Laney glared intensely at Deacon, holding her finger to her lips. Deacon brought his hand to his mouth, embarrassed that he had forgotten her one rule almost immediately.

They crept through the living room, searching for hints of the location of the key. Suddenly, a voice emerged from the kitchen.

"I'm telling you," Tonya said. "Someone's stealing from us again. They're doing it right under our noses."

The group scurried to the next room, in what appeared to be a dining room. There was a long table with an overly decorated chandelier dangling above. A pristine collection of porcelain dishware sat on display in a large cabinet against the wall. There were decorative plates with intricate blue patterns and light gold trimming. One of the plates was at the head of the table, smeared with a gravy-like substance. Laney pressed her back against the wall and listened to the voices around the corner.

"I hate to admit it," Joe said, sauntering into the living room and plopping onto the couch, "but maybe you're right."

"I know I'm right. We went for supplies just a few days ago, and we're already running low. You know just as well as everyone else that each trip to New Valley is a huge risk. The place is swarming with clunkers."

"I know." Joe threw his arms over his head, resting his interlocked fingers on the crown of his scalp. "It's so hard to find people you can trust. It's like we have a new thief every month."

"What are you going to do about it?"

"We have to find out who it is first. And then we punish them."

Tonya wandered to the couch and nuzzled next to him. "Drive them out and shoot them like the others?"

"No. This will just keep happening unless we handle it differently. We need to show them what happens when you mess with Joe Hannigan."

"You mean a public execution," Tonya confirmed.

"That's right. It's the only way to keep them in line."

"I still don't know why we need them at all. It seems to me like we're better off on our own. Just the four of us. Fewer mouths to feed."

"I've already explained this. We need expendable manpower. When a squad of clunkers comes knocking on our door, we need a few goons to throw their way. It's how Caesar built his empire. Strength in numbers. Expendable manpower."

"Caesar was stabbed to death in a room full of traitors."

"True, but we're not an empire. I can handle ten guys."

Two more people entered the room.

"Hey, Joe," one of them said. His voice was softer than Joe's. "We're ready for tomorrow, but we can't find the key. Have you seen it around?"

"You lost the key?" Tonya said. "You're such a klutz, Terry."

"It wasn't my fault, Joe. Your sister had it last."

A fourth voice spoke. A woman. "I didn't lose the key. I gave it to Terry."

Terry moved in front of the couch to face Joe, but he kept his eyes locked on Valerie. "I think I would remember that, Val. Don't insult my intelligence." He shifted his eyes to Joe. "Your sis thinks I'm an idiot, but I swear to God, I didn't lose it. I distinctly remember giving it back to her. You believe me, right, buddy?"

Joe stood up from the couch. "Frankly, I don't give a crap who had the key last. We're low on supplies. We need to go back to New Valley. Just find that key before morning."

"And if we can't find it?" Terry asked.

"You *will* find it. Go upstairs and keep looking. Tear your rooms apart if you have to."

"It's not going to be up there."

"Shut your mouth and listen to my brother," Val said. "Go now. I'll be up in a minute."

Terry shrugged. "Okay. Whatever you say, boss. But we're wasting our time. I think one of our other guys has it."

"Shut up and go, Terry," Val said even louder.

Terry scurried up the stairs, mumbling to himself as he whizzed past Laney on the other side of the wall.

"I don't know why we keep him around," Val said. "He's always screwing things up."

"He's a good friend," Joe said. "You know that. I've known him since grade school."

"I've known him just as long, and I've never liked him."

Tonya twisted around on the couch to face Val. "Is it because he tried to kiss ya in high school?"

Val scrunched her face, startled by the question.

"Joe told me," Tonya said. "Sixteen-year-old Terry had a crush on you back in the day."

"And you managed to ignore him for most of high school," Joe added.

"That's right," Tonya said with a huge smirk. "And then on prom night, the poor guy finally made his move. Tried to smooch ya right on the lips."

"And I socked him in the nose," Val said.

Joe shook his head, tilting his hat downward. "I don't know if he'll ever get over that night."

"Good," Val said with a cold stare. "I want him to know there's never a chance."

"But the past is the past," Joe said. "If you two can't get along, that's not my problem. Terry's one of the three people I trust, and he's not leaving anytime soon. Now, go up and help him find that key."

Val nodded and started toward the stairs but stopped halfway. "You know, there is a chance he's right. One of the others might've taken it."

Tonya hopped off the couch and pointed at Joe. "See? She thinks they're stealing from us, too."

Joe pulled her back to the couch and threw his arm over her shoulder. "Sure, there's a chance one of them stole it, but if they did, they would have bailed by now. Last time I checked, the car's still in the garage. I do believe someone is stealing food. I'll deal with them later, but right now, finding that key is our priority. No key means no car, and no car means no more trips to New Valley."

"Right," Val said, reaching the base of the stairs. "Don't worry. Terry and I will find it."

She climbed the steps, leaving Joe and Tonya alone on the couch. The miniature speakers were now playing "When the Man Comes Around." The tips of their boots tapped together as they listened to the gruff tone of Johnny Cash's voice.

Laney leaned around the corner. The couple was facing away from the stairs. Without speaking, she pointed to Silas and Amber, and then to the stairs. Amber nodded and tiptoed out of the dining room, keeping her eye on the back of Joe and Tonya's heads.

Silas followed with his hand on his holster. He turned the corner and peered up the length of the stairs. The top half of the stairwell was shrouded in darkness. He lifted his foot to take the first step, but his toe caught the edge and he stumbled toward the ground.

Amber hunched over, catching him just in time to prevent a symphony of noise. An uncontrolled groan escaped her mouth as she hoisted him back up. They froze in place, praying that Joe and Tonya hadn't heard. Tonya adjusted her posture but stayed facing the other way. She plucked off Joe's hat to run her fingers through his thick brown hair and then settled her head into the fold of his arm.

With a silent sigh of relief, Amber glared at Silas and pointed to the handrail. She grabbed it with her own hand to demonstrate. Silas nodded and grabbed it as well.

They climbed the stairs to the second floor, where the sound of Johnny Cash was just a distant echo. Silas's holster scratched against his hip. He pressed the side of his gun to muffle the sound as they walked. The dark corridor was illuminated only by the faint glow of a room on the right and another at the far end on the left.

Without warning, Terry emerged from the room on the right. He turned his back to Amber and Silas and marched down the hallway. Silas froze, not daring to look down at Amber, but assuming she had done the same. They stood like statues in the middle of the hallway as Terry walked away from them.

"It's not in there!" Terry yelled. "We're wasting our time, Val. I'm telling you, one of the guys has it. I don't trust a single one of them. What we should be doing is keeping an eye on the garage. They're bound to take a shot at the car eventually."

Val's voice came from the room on the left. "Joe says to keep looking, so that's what we do. You forget that my brother's in charge. What he says goes. Period. Now quit whining and get back to work."

"I don't forget he's in charge. I just think there should be a little democracy going on here."

"That kind of thing doesn't work. We've tried it already, and you know how that turned out. What we need is a leader, and we all agreed that Joe is the best fit for the job."

"Yeah, well, I think the power's getting to his head." He turned the corner to enter her room.

The hallway was clear. Silas and Amber snaked along the wall and slipped into Terry's room. Judging from the décor, it had once been a child's bedroom. The floor was littered with toy cars and trucks. The wallpaper showcased a series of racecars zooming from wall to wall, and the bed frame was a red sports car. The headlight decals were peeling off, and the flame patterns on the sides were almost completely faded.

The room was lit by a kerosene lantern next to the window. Amber peered through the glass. Joe and Tonya were crossing the walkway and entering the yard next door.

"They're going to the other house," she whispered. "That should give Laney and Marsh some room to explore downstairs." The volume of Terry and Val's chatter grew as they traveled back down the hall.

"Unfortunately, we still have to deal with these two. They're coming back." She pointed to the closet. "Quick, hide in there."

Silas shuffled into the closet, and Amber stuffed in next to him. They swung the door shut as Terry and Val entered the room. Through a small crack, they watched.

"You're not looking hard enough," Val said. "Are you even trying to find the key?"

Terry walked up to her with his hands on his hips. "What do you mean I'm not looking hard enough?"

"You should be tearing this room apart." She kicked a toy garbage truck out of the way. "Move some of this crap, at least."

"Hey, show some respect. These were once the cherished toys of a young boy. They're relics of joy. Not that you would know anything about joy."

"What is that supposed to mean?"

Terry shrugged. "I'm just saying, there's a reason the guys call you Queen Bitch, and it's not because they're David Bowie fans."

"I don't care what the guys call me, and neither should you. Your only concern should be finding the key." She kicked another toy, this time a cement truck. The plastic mixing drum popped off and rolled in front of the closet. "Now, clear out this trash and actually look this time. Hell, flip over that dumb bed if you have to."

"Dumb? I think it's kind of cool."

"That's not surprising at all."

"You just don't appreciate the wonder of childhood memories. I was way into cars when I was little."

"I don't care about your childhood, Terry. Find the key. We don't stop until we find it."

"Yeah, yeah, I know."

"I better not see your face again unless you have the key."

She stormed out and stomped down the hallway. Terry let out an exasperated sigh and plopped down on a chair by the window, his back to the closet.

Amber tapped Silas's shoulder. "You stay here," she whispered. "I'll follow Val." Before Silas could protest, she pushed open the door and slipped out of the room.

Silas pulled the door back shut and stared at Terry through the crack.

The heavyset man was tapping his fingers on the wooden desk. He started to hum the melody from "Folsom Prison Blues" but stopped halfway through the first verse. "Joe's really got to get some new songs. That jam's going to drive me mad." After a moment of silence, he started to hum again, this time embracing the melody.

Continuing his search for the coveted key, he pulled open one of the desk drawers and halfheartedly flipped through the trinkets inside. "Nothing in here," he said to himself. "What a surprise." He moved to the drawer below. Another moment of digging, and then he shook his head and shut the drawer, standing up to scan the room. "Where haven't I looked yet?" He stepped over a clutter of toys and toward the closet.

Silas backed away from the door as the man marched closer. He frantically searched the inside of the closet. The space was small with nowhere to hide. He pulled a folded blanket from the shelf and draped it over himself, pressing against the back wall.

The door creaked open, and light flooded in. Terry stood in the opening with his hands on his hips. "Jeez, this kid was messy." He started pulling items from the shelf and throwing them over his shoulder. "What are you doing, Terry?" he asked himself. "It's not going to be in this stupid closet. But Queen Bitch insists, so why not?"

Silas remained frozen to the wall, just barely able to see the man through the stitching of the blanket. The man's silhouette was exaggerated by the dramatic backlighting of the kerosene lantern. His face was hidden in shadow, but Silas could tell from the tone of his voice that he was irritated.

"Who does she think she is, ordering me around like that? Joe's in charge, not her. Sure, she's his sister, but I'm his best friend. I'm just as close as she is." He finished going through the top shelf and moved to the one below it. "If anything, I should be giving *her* orders. I'm older. I have seniority."

He finished with the second shelf and moved to the ones near the bottom, crouching down on one knee. Silas was now at eye level with the man and could see his face more clearly. His stubble. His aged wrinkles. His wild hair.

"I'm closer to Joe than she ever was. Just because she's family, she thinks she gets to boss everyone around. Well, newsflash, lady. He doesn't even like you that much. The only reason he keeps you around is *because* you're related. If you weren't, you'd be shacked up next door with the rest of those idiots. Or dead in a ditch somewhere."

He moved a shelf lower, placing a hand on Silas's head for balance. He leaned closer, and the blanket shifted, exposing Silas's foot.

He won't look down, Silas thought. *If I'm lucky, he won't look down.*

"Me, on the other hand," Terry muttered. "I've earned my spot in the group. I've been loyal to Joe from the day we met. She hasn't earned anything. She just sits around and does whatever she wants. Well, screw her."

He grabbed the blanket and threw it across the room, turning away as he did so. Silas sat completely exposed, watching Terry stomp around.

"This time, I won't let her get away with it." He rubbed his knuckles and stormed out.

The room was empty. Silas finally rose to his feet and emerged from the closet, standing in the middle of the mess that Terry had made. With Terry gone, now was his chance to look for the key. He approached the desk, opened the drawers from top to bottom, and rummaged through the papers inside. Nothing.

Next, he moved to the dresser, pulling out shirts and moving socks. Halfway through, he stopped to think. Why would the key be in a dresser? He had to be smart. Terry would be back any minute. The man had already searched the room. It wouldn't be out in the open, but maybe it had fallen behind something.

He returned to the desk and ran his hand along the smooth surface, moving toward the back and digging his fingers between the desk and the wall. The gap was tight, but wide enough for a key to slide through.

He knelt down and placed his head on the floor to look underneath. Dirt and dust was all he could see. He got to his feet and again wedged his fingers into the gap, this time pulling the desk away from the wall. Peeking behind, he could see nothing of interest.

From the hallway, he heard Val's voice. "You're such a pathetic loser. You know that, Terry?"

"Jeez!" Terry yelled. "Let go of me, Val." The clunk of their footsteps moved closer.

Silas crouched and searched for a place to hide. The closet was too far away. Instead, he scurried behind a tall wicker chair beside the dresser, peeking through the gaps in the weave.

Val and Terry stumbled in. Val held a tight grip on Terry's arm, pushing him forward as they walked. A red hue filled Terry's face and drool dribbled from his mouth.

"Seniority?" Val yelled. "You think you have seniority over me? Tell that to my brother. He would get a real kick out of it."

"Please, Val. You're going to break my arm."

"Maybe I should. You're disobeying a direct order from Joe. You know that, right? Find the key. Those were his words. So, if you want to keep those brains of yours, I would listen to orders and find the key. Otherwise, we can put you down like the mutt you are."

She shoved him to the ground and drew her sidearm, pressing the barrel against his forehead. Tears were running down his face.

"Just a pull of the trigger," she said, smiling. "That's all it takes, and then, bye-bye brains." She held the weapon against his skin for a moment longer, and then lowered it away. "Now get back to work, you pathetic clod." She holstered her gun and left the room.

Terry crawled across the floor and leaned up against the wall, his legs splayed and his back slouched. He wiped away the snot from his nose, but more oozed out.

Silas watched from behind the chair, waiting to see what the man would do next. But he did nothing. He just sat in total silence. Silas turned his attention back to the gap he had exposed from pulling the desk out. From this new angle, it was clear that the key was not there.

He was turning back to Terry when a sharp glint from behind the dresser caught his eye. It was a key, dangling from a loose nail on the back face of the dresser. It had fallen from the top and was now teetering precariously between the dresser and the wall.

Terry was still pouting. His tear-glazed eyes were in a daze, staring down at the floor. It was like he was in a trance, unaware of his surroundings. Silas leaned out with his arm extended, nudging the edge of the dresser with his finger. The key swayed at the tip of the nail, ready to fall at any moment.

He leaned out a little more when a dull thump startled him. He retreated behind the chair and moved his attention back to Terry.

The man was hitting his head against the wall. "You're such a coward," he said to himself.

Thump. The key wobbled more.

"You're such a useless moron."

Thump. Thump. Thump.

"You're a worthless pile of scum who doesn't deserve to live." He raised his arm over his head and shoved his elbow into the wall.

With this last thump, the key hopped off the nail and fell to the ground. Silas cringed at the distinct clink of the metal object landing on the hardwood floor. The key bounced off the wall and tumbled into plain sight.

Terry stopped, wiped the tears from his eyes, and turned his head toward the sound. There, sitting right next to him, was the key. He reached out and held it in his fingertips, letting the flame of the kerosene lantern dance in its reflection. His gaping mouth slowly formed a joyous smile. "Maybe you're not so useless after all, Mr. Schwartz."

The pop of a gunshot rang down the hall. Terry flinched at the sound, shoving the key into his pocket and scurrying out of the room.

Silas moved toward the door and poked his head out. He saw Terry peering into the other flame-lit room. A bustle of shadows stretched through the doorway and landed on the wall behind him. Muffled grunts and groans escaped the room.

"Holy crap!" Terry yelled, rushing in.

Silas slipped into the hallway and briskly walked toward the sound of commotion. He pulled out his revolver, dreading the possibility of having to use it. The struggle grew louder as he drew closer. When he turned the corner, he did not enter, but watched from the hallway instead.

Val was flailing around the room with Amber clinging to her back. Amber's gun had been tossed into a pile of clothes. Val reached for her own gun, but Amber kicked the holster. It popped off her belt and slid across the floor.

"Don't just stand there!" Val screamed. "Get the girl off of me, you idiot!"

"What if I don't?" Terry asked, standing off to the side.

"What the hell are you talking about, Terry? Shut up and do something useful for once!"

"Do something useful?" he repeated, pulling the key from his pocket. "How is *this* for useful, huh?"

"Jesus Christ, Terry." She thrashed around, slamming Amber into a wall. "This is not the time."

Amber let go for a brief moment, but hopped back on, squeezing even tighter. Pulling back on Val's neck, she unsheathed her knife and sunk it into her shoulder. Val shrieked. Amber pulled it out, raised up her arm, and plunged it back down again.

"Who's the pathetic clod now?" Terry asked, holding his arms out. "Joe said to find the key, and I'm the one who found it. Meanwhile, some pre-teen brat is kicking your ass. Joe doesn't need you. He never needed you. He only kept you around because you're his sister, but we all know he wants you gone. The group is better off without you."

Val's eyes flared with rage. "You're done, Terry. I'm going to make your life a living hell."

Amber stabbed her two more times, closer to the chest.

"I have a hard time believing that," Terry said, "unless you plan on haunting me from the grave. Now, shut up and die."

Amber sunk the knife once more, this time hitting her heart. Val's body stiffened as the metal pierced her skin. She fell forward, bouncing her head off a desk and hitting the floor.

With Val dead, Amber let go and turned toward Terry.

"Good job, kid," Terry said, flashing a smile. "You just took care of the biggest pain in my ass." He reached for his gun. "Now it's your turn."

Amber pointed the knife at him. "Try me," she said, unfazed.

Terry glanced at the knife and laughed. "Kid, haven't you heard the phrase, *don't bring a knife to a gunfight*? I know you're young, but you should know better."

Amber nodded. "I've heard it a few times, but I have some better advice."

Terry smiled at the girl's confidence. "You do, huh? And what would that be?"

"Don't bring a gun to a simmi fight." She pointed to Silas, who entered from the shadows.

Terry fell back as Silas stepped forward. "Holy hell, a clunker." He scurried to the back wall. "You know this thing?"

Amber retrieved her gun and hopped up onto the desk, sitting next to the blood-stained edge where Val had bashed her head. "Not only do I know him. I work with him."

"Jesus Christ, kid. Working with a clunker? You're really playing with fire, you know that?"

Amber turned to Silas. "Get that key from him, would you, buddy?"

Terry raised his gun. "Don't come any closer. I'll blow your circuits out. I swear to God, I will."

Ignoring his threats, Silas stepped forward. The gun fired, sending a bullet at his chest. It ricocheted off, leaving no more than a dent. He pointed his six-shooter downward and fired.

Terry dropped, screaming with pain. He rolled on the floor, grabbing his leg as blood seeped through the leg of his pants.

"Drop the gun," Silas said. The confidence in his voice was a pleasant surprise.

"Okay, man," Terry pleaded, placing his gun on the floor. "Whatever you say. Just don't kill me."

Amber hopped off the desk and zigzagged around Val's body to kneel beside Terry. She stuck out her hand and smiled. "Key, please."

Terry fumbled for the key and handed it over.

"I'll take the gun, too," Amber said, reaching over and grabbing it. "Thanks, dude. It was a pleasure doing business with you. Now, if you don't mind, we have a car to steal." She stood up and turned around. "Let's go. The others should be waiting for—"

Terry leapt across the floor, reaching for Val's holster. He pulled the weapon from its leather pouch and pointed the barrel at Amber's head.

Silas reacted. His arm sprung forward, and he pulled the trigger. A bullet shot from the old revolver, past Amber's cheek and through the bridge of Terry's nose. His head snapped back, and a spatter of blood hit the wall. His arms fell and the gun gently rolled from his hand. A single crimson drop oozed down and gathered at the tip of his nose.

Amber winced at the sound of the shot, clasping her hands over her ears. She glanced up at the smoking barrel and twisted around to look at Terry. His dead eyes glared at the wall behind her.

"That was amazing," she said, hopping with excitement. "This dude was terrified of you. Just one look and his knees were shaking."

Silas pointed to Val. "What happened? I heard gunshots."

"She saw me, so I drew my gun. She hit it out of my hand and it went off. With that, and the two shots you fired, we've made quite a ruckus. Let's bail before the cavalry arrives."

"To the garage?" Silas asked, sliding the gun back in his holster.

"That's the plan, man. Get to the garage, start up the car, and get the hell out of Dodge."

"Dodge?"

"You need to watch more Westerns, dude."

"That's what Deacon says."

"Really?" Amber asked, bending down to scoop up Val's gun. "Marsh is a Western man, huh? *Gunsmoke. Rawhide. Bonanza.* Laney and I found a whole collection a while back, with a working VHS player and everything. I watched them over and over until the damn tube blew out. There's this one Clint Eastwood flick where he shoots a noose. Saves a guy from the gallows. It's exciting stuff. Although, I doubt that could happen in real life."

"You would be surprised," Silas said, examining his gun and imagining the precise aim it would require to shoot a rope. Difficult? Yes. Impossible? Maybe not.

"My favorite was *The Rifleman*," she said. "Chuck Connors wielding a kick-ass lever-action rifle." She tossed the key to Silas. "Here, I've never driven before."

"Neither have I."

"Maybe Laney or Marsh knows how. Come on. Let's go."

Silas tucked the key in his holster and followed her through the hallway. They crept down the stairs, moving quickly and quietly at the same time. When they reached the bottom, the back door swung open and two men entered the living room. Silas and Amber slipped into the dining room.

"I didn't hear a thing," said one of the men. His voice was soft and monotone. "You're all just paranoid."

"How did you not hear it?" a second voice responded. This one was high and nasally. "It woke the entire house."

"I was sitting right by the window. If there was a gunshot, I would have heard it."

"You're going deaf, Hank. Even Joe heard it. And now he wants us to investigate. So, shut up and do your job."

"Why can't he check it out himself? It's his house. It's like we're not allowed in here unless there's danger."

"Weren't you listening? He's checking the garage. Right now, the car's our biggest asset."

"And he doesn't trust us enough to lay a finger on it. I'm surprised he lets us even look at it."

"If you have a problem with the way he operates, bring it up with him. I'm tired of hearing you complain behind his back."

The men turned the corner and climbed the stairs to the second floor. Their voices faded to distant echoes.

Amber pulled on Silas's arm. "Joe's on his way to the garage. We're going to miss our chance to snag the car."

They passed the stairwell and entered the living room. The speakers were no longer playing the upbeat music of Johnny Cash. Now, there was only silence, with the subtle thump of footsteps above.

As they approached the back door, Amber glimpsed through the window. There were two men outside. She crouched, pulling Silas beside her, and poked her head up again. The men were standing on either side of the door, armed with automatic rifles. Two others patrolled the yard, circling the sludge-filled pool.

Amber shook her head and spun around. "Not this way. Try the front door."

They backtracked through the living room, peeking up the stairs as they passed. The men on the second floor were still occupied. As they approached the front, Silas could hear muffled voices through the door.

This time he held Amber back. "Not this way either."

The girl nodded in agreement. "We sure drew a lot of attention to ourselves. I guess a few gunshots will do that."

"What now?" Silas asked.

Before Amber could answer, the two voices upstairs reemerged.

"Joe is going to be pissed," said the nasally voice. Their feet clopped down the stairs.

"You think I don't know that, William? His best friend and his sister are dead, and whoever killed them is roaming around out there. Why in the world would he not be pissed?"

Amber nudged Silas, pointing to the window on the far wall. They glided through the living room, toward their only escape.

"He's going to be pissed at *us*," the first voice continued. "And he has a reputation for shooting the messenger."

"You're overreacting. He's not going to shoot us." Their voices grew louder.

"It's a figure of speech, Hank. I know he's not going to shoot us, but he's going to give us hell."

Amber slid open the window, letting in a cool gust of air. "You first," she whispered.

Silas did not protest. He sat on the sill, swung his legs through, and dropped into a patch of overgrown grass. He reached up to help Amber, but she had already landed beside him.

"It's chilly in here," said the voice from inside. "Shut the window, will you?"

Amber trotted away from the window, toward the street, and Silas followed.

AND EXECUTE

SILAS AND AMBER lurked through the darkness and regrouped by a mailbox across the street, watching the dimly lit house from a distance. Guards had swarmed the house like mosquitoes to an open flame. A dozen in sight. Half at various entrances of the house and half surrounding the garage.

"That's not good for Laney and Marsh," Amber said. She checked her wristwatch. "Just over fifteen minutes. They were probably waiting for us when the guns went off."

"And Joe's in there with them," Silas said.

"We drew them in with a gunshot. We can do the same to draw them out." She pulled out her gun. "I'll run down the street and fire off a few shots. That should get their attention."

"But then they'll be after you."

"Don't worry about me. I can handle myself. Your job is to find Laney and Marsh and bust out with that car. I'll wait for you down the street. Pick me up, and then we're home free."

"We shouldn't split up again."

"It's not ideal, but we have no other choice. We need a distraction, and a gun is the best we have."

"Or something that sounds like a gun," Silas said, digging through his bag.

"What are you talking about?"

"All we need is a delayed loud noise."

"What, do you have a remote mine in there or something?"

"Not quite," he said, pulling out a water bottle. "Have you ever heard of an MRE?"

Amber cocked her head to the side. "No. What's an MRE?"

Silas placed the water bottle down and continued to dig through his bag. "It stands for Meal, Ready-to-Eat. It's a meal specifically made for military use. They're compact, lightweight, and long-lasting."

"Okay," Amber said, more perplexed than before. "How does that help us, exactly?"

Silas pulled out one of the boxes and held it up to show her. "We found these a while back. Of course, I don't have to eat, but Deacon was pretty excited to have a hot meal."

"Hot meal? It just looks like a normal box of food to me."

"Yes, it does, but there's more to it. Add a little water, and a chemical reaction heats up the food." He turned the box to show her the front. "This one is chicken fajita."

"So, we can heat up food. What's the big deal?"

"Let me finish. When we found these, we learned two things. First, they taste pretty bad. I think Deacon's exact words were *vomit in a box*. He refuses to eat them. I just keep them for emergencies."

"I get it, man. We have a bunch of barf-flavored food. Get to the point."

"The second thing we learned, thanks to our own carelessness, is that the chemical reaction can build quite a bit of pressure. Contain that pressure in something like a bear canister, or anything airtight," he picked up the water bottle, "and it creates a pretty loud noise."

Amber's eyes widened. "You don't say. And it sounds like a gunshot?"

"Almost identical."

"I got to say, simulated or not, you're one intelligent dude." She grabbed the MRE from Silas and flipped it over to read the instructions. "How does it work?"

Silas pulled out another box. Chicken pesto pasta. "There should be something called a *heater* in there. The powder is what causes the reaction."

Amber tore off the top of the box and removed the pouch labeled *MRE Heater*. "Is this it?"

Silas nodded and opened his own box, removing the same pouch. They ripped them open and looked inside.

"It looks like gunpowder," Silas said.

"That probably means we've got the right stuff." Amber grabbed her own bottle of water. "How much water do we need?"

"Not a lot. But don't mix it yet. We should prepare some more and use them all at once."

"I like the way you think."

They lined up four bottles and rationed out the water. Silas found two more MREs. Beef ravioli and lemon pepper tuna. They removed the heaters and prepared the powder.

"So," Amber said, holding a bottle in one hand and a pouch in the other, "we just pour this stuff in and put on the cap?"

"Yes," Silas answered, reaching for his own bottle. "Make sure it's airtight. That part's important."

"Easy enough. How long does it take?"

"Back at the camp, it took about ten minutes."

"Plenty of time," she said, dumping the powder into the bottle and tightening the cap. A fizzing noise seeped through the plastic, and bubbles started to form. "Where do we put them?"

"We should have figured that out before you mixed it."

"As long as the noise is away from the garage, it should work. Let's just throw them down the street."

Silas looked in both directions. "Which way?"

"Does it matter? It's not like—" She pulled back her hand and dropped the fizzing bottle. The inside was filled with a cloud of white gas, and the sides were starting to bulge. "Jeez, that thing's getting hot. Are you sure we have ten minutes? It looks like it's ready to blow."

Silas shrugged. "At the camp it—"

The bottle erupted, sending plastic shrapnel in every direction. The sudden noise startled both of them. Silas stumbled a few steps back, and Amber fell over completely.

She jumped to her feet and darted her attention to the guards by the house. They were all looking in Silas and Amber's direction, and one was walking over. "Crap!" she whispered, reaching for another bottle. "Quick. Mix some more. They definitely heard that, but I think it's too dark for them to see us. We can toss the rest over there."

Silas mixed another bottle, glancing at the approaching guard. The man was already halfway across the street, peering right at them but blinded by darkness. Silas wound his arm back and launched the concoction three houses down.

Amber watched the noisemaker soar as she crafted a brand-new one. She placed a third and fourth in Silas's hand and watched them fly through the sky.

They waited, hidden only by the thick veil of night. The guard moved closer, stepping past the yellow striping with his rifle up. Amber and Silas both crouched, Amber holding her breath and Silas covering the light on his shoulder. The guard stopped at the curb, leaning forward and straining his eyes.

There was another eruption of sound down the street. It was distant, but loud enough to grab the guard's attention. He turned, both startled and curious. Then, two more bursts in rapid succession. "It's coming from over there!" he yelled. "They must be a few houses down. Let's go check it out."

"Joe said to stay here," said one of the others.

"Because he thinks we've got them trapped in the garage, but someone's shooting over there, and it isn't one of our guys."

"Joe will be pissed if we leave."

"He'll be pissed if whoever's on a shooting spree gets away."

The other guard hesitated, and then nodded. "Just four of us," he said, waving at two others to follow. He pointed at the two by the door. "The two of you stay here."

The four guards wandered off, leaving only two in the front yard.

"It worked," Amber said, standing up. "I can't believe it actually worked."

Silas shook his head. "I don't know what happened. Back at the camp, the fuse time was much longer."

"Whatever, dude. Your plan worked. We need to get moving before the others come back."

Silas pointed to the far side of the garage. "We can go around that way."

"That's exactly what I was thinking."

She scrambled across the street, leading the way to the garage.

They hid behind a fence, peeking over the top to see the side entrance of the garage. A smudged window displayed the fuzzy view of the space inside. It was hard to see, but there was the vague shape of a vehicle.

"The car," Amber said. "We're so close."

"Joe is in there. Deacon and Laney might be as well."

"Right. First, we check on Laney and Marsh. Then we can worry about the car."

They hopped the fence and approached the door. Silas rose to peek through the window. To his left was the car. It was a bland beige tint with only mild scratches. On the roof was a yellow sign that read *STUDENT DRIVER*.

To his right, he saw Deacon and Laney against the wall. Their guns were drawn and pointed outward. Joe, Tonya, and two other men stood in a circle around them, pointing back with their own guns.

"Uh-oh," Silas said.

Amber poked her head up to see. "Crap. That's not good."

She entered the room, and Silas followed, making sure the door didn't slam behind them. They ducked behind the back of the car and slowly moved toward the front.

"Just give up," Joe said with his revolver aimed at Deacon. "You're outnumbered."

"We've got dozens of others," Deacon said. "And it sounds like they've been giving your guys a hard time out there."

"I don't care what's happening out there. In here, right now, it's just two against four. It's pretty clear who gets out alive."

"The cavalry's coming, Joe, and it's going to be one hell of a rodeo when they get here."

"Shut up!" Tonya yelled. "You need to learn some respect." She turned to Joe. "You should have killed these two when you had the chance."

"That *was* the plan," Joe said, staring at Deacon. "But Charlie and Connor went and screwed it up. They deserved what they got. Those idiots were always useless. What happened to the clunker that was with you? You kill him too? Serves him well. He wouldn't have lasted long on his own."

"And you," Tonya said, staring at Laney. "You're just a regular Houdini, aren't you? One day you're tied up, and the next day, poof, you're gone."

Amber and Silas emerged from hiding, remaining behind the four hostiles. Deacon and Laney briefly glanced up and then shifted their eyes back to Joe.

"You're certainly smarter than this piece of scum," Joe said, pointing to Deacon. "But where's the girl? Is *she* the cavalry? Is *she* the dozens that are on their way?"

"Okay," Deacon said lowering his gun. "You called my bluff. The girl is the only backup we have."

Laney turned to Deacon. "What are you doing?"

Amber and Silas raised their guns, aiming at Joe and Tonya's heads.

"It's okay, Laney. Lower your weapon." He pushed her gun down. "Let's face it. We don't stand a chance. We came for the car, and we've failed. But let me ask you one question, Joe. Do you play golf?"

Joe leaned in. "What the hell are you talking about?"

"I was never a golf man myself. I couldn't get the swing right. It was the funniest thing. I played baseball in high school. Never had trouble swinging a bat, but a golf club is an entirely different story. Half of the time I would miss the damn ball, and if I made contact, the thing would nosedive fifty feet out. I just couldn't get the hang of it."

Tonya turned to Joe. "Don't listen to this idiot. Let's just shoot them and get this over with."

Joe responded with baffled silence.

"Now, mini golf," Deacon said, placing his gun down. "Mini golf is where I shine. The windmill. The pirate ship. The giant terrifying clown head that opens and closes its mouth. Yup. Take me out mini golfing and I'm unstoppable."

Joe smiled. "Hmm, is that so?"

"Yes, sir, and I don't mean to brag, but I once shot a perfect game at Willy West's. You know, that cowboy joint. My daughter saw me do it. When I hit that final hole in one, her face lit up like a pack of cigars. She asked me what my secret was, and I told her it's easy. It's all about the angle. Simple geometry. All you have to do is plan out your shot, aim, and execute."

These words drew Silas's attention.

"That's all there is to it. Plan, aim, and execute. Just line it up, get the right angle, and pull the trigger."

Joe cocked his head. "Pull the what?"

Four shots fired from Silas's gun. Four bodies fell like bags of meat. The hat on Joe's head popped off and tumbled to the ground.

"Jesus Christ!" Amber said, admiring the precision of Silas's aim. He had placed a single bullet between each of their eyes. "That was crazy. You dropped all four before I could shoot once."

Equally impressed, Laney stared at the smoking revolver. "You're one hell of a shot. But I guess I shouldn't have expected any less. You are a simmi, after all. I'm just glad you're on our side."

Deacon searched Joe's pockets. "No key."

Silas pulled the key from his holster. "I have it."

"He continues to impress," Laney said, walking to the car.

Silas tossed the key to Deacon.

"I doubt the auto-drive works," Deacon said. "I haven't driven a car in forever. Have you, Laney?"

"Not since my late twenties."

Deacon shrugged. "It'll come back. It's like riding a bike, right?"

"I can't ride a bike," Amber and Laney said together.

Deacon turned to Silas. "I assume you can't ride a bike either."

Silas shook his head. "I've never tried."

"Well, I guess I'm driving, then."

The side door of the garage burst open and a man charged in, screaming and waving his weapon. Silas aimed his gun and pulled the trigger, but the anticipated shot was met with an empty click.

The man fired off a single shot, nicking Silas's leg before Laney filled his chest with lead. "Hurry!" she yelled. "The rest will be here any minute."

They scrambled into the car, Deacon taking the driver's seat. Silas got in on the passenger's side, surprised to see a second steering wheel. With no time for questions, he hopped in and slammed the door.

Deacon held up the key. "The moment of truth. Are you ready?"

Amber dealt a swift kick to the back of his seat. "Quit stalling and start the damn thing."

He slid the key in and turned his wrist. The engine wheezed along at first and then grew to a steady rumble. "Hallelujah, it works!" he cheered. "Here we go."

"Wait," Amber said, hopping out. When she reappeared, she held a flexible plastic tube. "To siphon gas."

"Good thinking." Deacon gripped the steering wheel and looked out of the windshield at the large garage door that was blocking their exit. "Someone needs to open the door."

Another guard entered from the side, firing his weapon in every direction. Laney's window exploded in shards. "Just go!" she yelled, ducking down and shielding her head. "Go! Go! Go!"

He shifted into drive and slammed on the gas. The steady rumble turned into a fierce roar, but the car remained where it was. Another bullet shattered Silas's side-view mirror. A third hit the roof-mounted sign. The smell of hot rubber began to fill the air.

"Silas, your foot!" Amber yelled, shouting over the engine.

Silas looked down to see that his foot was pushing against the passenger's side brake pedal. He lifted it up and the car jolted forward, ramming the garage door off of its rollers and bursting through to the other side.

A body slammed into the front of the car, rolling onto the hood and sliding off. Deacon swerved to the left, off the driveway and onto the grass. Another man stood in their way, pointing his gun and shooting through the windshield. Deacon spun the wheel to the right and slammed on the break, swinging the back of the car into the guard. He pushed on the gas and straightened the wheel. They shot off the curb and landed on asphalt, roaring down the street with nothing left in their way.

Amber twisted her body around to look through the back window. "We did it!" she said. "We actually did it." She stuck her head out into the wind and cheered.

Deacon honked the horn in victory, adrenaline pumping through his body. "You're damn right, we did! We snuck in and ripped them apart from the inside. We're like the Greeks. Breaking into Troy and stealing their goddamn horse."

Laney held an amused grin. "That's not quite what happened in Troy."

"Who cares about Troy? We have a fricking car. And it actually works. How awesome is that?"

"It's pretty fricking awesome," Amber said. She leaned forward to pat Silas on the shoulder. "And the MVP of the night is this guy."

Deacon nodded. "I've got to admit, you impressed me back there. You handled yourself like a real cowboy, taking out Joe and the others. I've never seen anyone shoot like that."

"He's a real Dirty Harry," Amber said. "He saved me from Terry, too. Put a bullet right through his brains."

Deacon glanced at Amber through the mirror. "You know Dirty Harry?"

"Sure, dude. Clint Eastwood as a badass cop. It's a classic. Speaking of which, Silas tells me you're a Western connoisseur. I think we need to educate our simmi in the ways of Clint Eastwood."

Deacon grinned. "I'm really starting to like this girl."

Laney nodded. "She's a doll, isn't she?"

"*Doll* isn't exactly the word I would choose, but I have a soft spot for anyone who likes a good Western. To be honest, I'm a little upset Joe Cowboy had to die. The man had pretty good taste. But alas, he's not our problem anymore, and it's all thanks to Silas."

Silas looked down at his revolver, flipping open the cylinder. Six empty slots. Six lead bullets that were now burrowed deep within the flesh of five lifeless bodies. To his surprise, he felt no remorse. Instead, there was a feeling of satisfaction. He loaded six more bullets, shut the cylinder, and packed the weapon into his holster.

And with that, they drove through the night in their beat-up car, moving away from town and hurtling toward the most dangerous place in the world. New Valley.

Road Trip

A MBER'S GENTLE SNORING and the low hum of the engine formed an oddly soothing ambiance. She had propped her cheek on the car door and curled her legs across the middle seat. Laney was sleeping as well, with her head tilted back and her mouth hanging open.

Silas peered out at the dry desert scenery as they rolled down the open highway. The cracks in the dirt reminded him of reptile skin. There was no vegetation. No signs of life. But despite the idea of a desert wasteland, there was still something beautiful about it all. Just the dirt and the sky, and nothing else.

Deacon kept his eyes on the road. "I really miss these long road trips," he said as they passed an interstate sign. "I used to take the family on cross-country road trips all the time. There's nothing better than cruising down the open road. These moments, when everyone's asleep and I'm driving, these are the moments to cherish. Just me, the road, and the low hum of that sweet engine. Nothing to think about. Nothing to stress about. Nothing to do but relax."

Silas continued to look out his window, admiring the view.

Deacon glanced over at the passenger's side. "Do you want to drive?"

Silas snapped out of his trance. "What?"

"I said, do you want to drive? You've got your own steering wheel on that side. Pedals too."

Silas slouched to see the two pedals by his feet. "I've never driven before."

"Well, we already have that student driver sign. You can be my student. Seeing how you shoot, this shouldn't be a problem for you. Just grab the wheel."

Silas did as he said, wrapping both hands around the wheel as Deacon let go.

"Good. Keep it straight. Stay in the lane. Now, I'm going to release the gas pedal so you can take over. It's the pedal on the right. Ready?"

Silas nodded, keeping his eyes on the road. For a brief moment, the hum of the engine stopped, leaving the car in a neutral roll. He moved his foot toward the right pedal and pushed down. The car jerked forward and began to speed up.

"Easy," Deacon said. "No need to stomp down on it. We don't want to wake the ladies. Just ease your foot down."

He lifted his foot to enter a steady coast.

"There you go. Easy as pie. It's fun, right?"

Silas guided the wheel to the right as the road started to curve. "It beats walking."

"Have you ever taken a road trip before?"

"Desmond and Paige have gone on a few, but I would usually stay back and take care of the house."

"That's a shame. Everyone should experience the joys of a road trip. I guess I'm the lucky fellow who gets to show you this great pastime."

Silas looked straight ahead at the mountain tips breaking the horizon. "It is quite nice. And much faster. At this rate, we should reach New Valley in a few days."

"And thanks to this car, we might actually make it there alive."

"You didn't think we would make it on foot?"

"I'll admit, when we first met, I didn't think you could do much of anything. No offense, but it was pretty clear you weren't designed for combat."

"No, I was built for companionship."

"Right, I know. But companionship won't get you far in a war zone. You can't blame me for having my doubts. Even so, I went along with it. You seemed harmless enough, and it was nice to have a goal for once. It's better to die for something than it is to live for nothing. That's the inspirational cliché my dad always spouted."

"It's wise advice."

"Yeah, he wasn't the smartest guy, but there were nuggets of wisdom. That's the one that always stuck with me. I like to help people when I can, but lately, it seems like everyone just wants to kill each other."

"People are just trying to survive now."

"I would like to believe that, but the stuff I've seen...the things people do to survive..." He trailed off, staring at the yellow line in the middle of the road. "When you came along, I saw someone worth helping. I knew I couldn't let that opportunity slip away. So, thank you."

Silas placed a hand on Deacon's shoulder. "I should be the one thanking you."

"It's been a bumpy ride, but it looks like we've finally found a streak of luck. Never in a million years did I think I would find a working car, but here I am, speeding down the highway with three new friends. Three!"

Silas glanced at Laney and Amber. "I'm happy we found them as well."

"And then there are the supplies in the trunk. I mean, what are the chances of that? Tonya thought some traitor was stealing all of their stuff, but it turns out they just forgot to empty the trunk. I don't necessarily believe in God, but there has to be someone looking out for us, right? It's like the universe saw all the trash we were crawling through and decided to give us a break."

"I'll take it," Silas said. "Here, take the wheel back. I need a break of my own."

As Deacon took control of the car, there was shuffling in the back seat, followed by a yawn. Amber sat up and stretched her arms. "Nothing like a good nap."

"You were out for a while," Deacon said, looking at her through the mirror.

"We haven't had much time to sleep. Scoping out Joe's house was a full-time job."

"Well, we have the car and Joe is dead, so get all of the sleep you want."

"And to think, you guys almost blew the whole thing when we first found you."

"Don't lie," Deacon said, smirking. "You couldn't have pulled it off without us."

"We couldn't have pulled it off without Silas," Amber said. "We probably could have gotten by without you."

"That may be true, but lucky for me, Silas and I are bundled together. If you want the simmi, you're stuck with me."

"You're our driver," Silas said.

"That's right. I know how to drive. I will proudly serve as chauffeur."

Amber smiled. "You're not our chauffeur. You're our captain, dude."

"Ah yes, you've dubbed me Captain Marsh."

Amber raised a saluting hand to her forehead. "Amber, reporting for duty, sir."

Deacon turned to Silas and raised his eyebrows. "What do *you* think of that?"

Silas responded with a blank stare.

"Salute, dude," Amber said. "Show your captain some respect. Like this." She held up her hand again to demonstrate.

Silas raised his own hand to mimic Amber's salute.

"At ease, soldiers," Deacon said, returning his eyes to the road. "We've still got a long ride ahead of us. I want my soldiers to be comfortable."

Amber leaned back in her seat. "Such a considerate captain."

"What in the world are the two of you talking about?" Laney asked in a groggy voice, rubbing her eyes and stretching her arms.

"Just messing around," Deacon said. "Did you sleep well?"

"Better than I have in a long time. Where are we?"

Amber glanced out the window. "In the middle of nowhere, from the looks of it."

"We're on the highway," Silas said. "Route 66, I believe."

"Yes," Deacon said. "Route 66. We're driving on a piece of U.S. history."

Laney smiled. "There's nothing quite like a good old-fashioned road trip."

Deacon's eyes lit up with joy. "I was just telling Silas about the joys of a road trip. The sun. The engine. The view."

"And what a gorgeous view it is," Laney said, sticking her hand through the now shattered window and letting the wind flow through her fingers.

Amber rolled down her own window, sticking out her head and letting her hair flutter. After a moment, she ducked back in. "I've heard about cars before, and I see plenty of dead ones, but I didn't know they could go this fast."

Deacon glanced at the speedometer, which had leveled out at seventy miles per hour. "This baby can go much faster, honey."

Amber turned to Laney for confirmation, as if such a claim were impossible.

Laney nodded. "It sure can. I'm willing to bet this thing can hit a hundred."

Amber's face lit up. "Well, now we have to try."

"Okay, kids," Deacon said. "Let's burn some rubber." He leaned forward and slammed on the gas.

An invisible force sucked them back into their seats as the vehicle raced down the empty road. The thunderous engine grew louder and louder. A flurry of wind flew in through the windows and slapped them in the face.

Deacon looked at the dashboard. The needle hit eighty. Then ninety. It passed a hundred and continued to climb. He cheered like a crazed lunatic. A hundred and ten. A hundred and twenty.

"One twenty!" he screamed. The engine was so loud that he had trouble hearing his own voice.

"What?" Laney mouthed, cupping a hand behind her ear.

The steering wheel started to wobble. Deacon tried to hold it in place, but its resistance was surprisingly strong. The car swayed from side to side, veering onto the dirt.

"Stay on the road!" Silas yelled, hoping Deacon could hear him over the engine.

"I'm trying!" he yelled back, slamming on the brake.

Momentum threw them forward. Their heads snapped down and their arms flew outward. Silas grabbed his seat, worried that the sheer force would send him through the windshield.

They swerved off the road, sliding onto the dry desert dirt. Dust kicked up and filled the air. They spun in frantic circles, leaving deep skid marks in the ground. The outward force swung Silas's head into the window. The window shattered, sending shards of glass at Amber in the backseat. She turned away and covered her face. The car slid a little further and finally came to a stop. More dust filled the car, followed by the smell of hot motor oil.

"Is everyone okay?" Deacon asked.

Amber plucked a small shard of glass out of her hair and tossed it out the window. "My heart might explode, but no scrapes or bruises."

Laney swatted at the dust particles. "I guess that's why most cars have auto-drive."

Deacon looked at the shattered window next to Silas. "What about you?"

Silas opened his door to step out. "I hit my head, but I'll be fine."

Deacon stepped out to examine the car. "A broken window and a few bullet holes from before. Nothing major." He moved to the front and tapped the hood. "But the engine. It didn't sound too good when we were revving up." He pointed to Laney. "Get the hood, would you?"

She reached below the driver's seat to pull the lever. A latch unhooked and the hood popped open. Deacon lifted it up and propped it open.

A thick cloud of dark smoke puffed up. They backed away as a scorching heat radiated from the engine.

"Jeez," Amber said. "The thing's hotter than a sauna. Is that supposed to happen?"

Deacon scratched his head. "Not unless you're trying to catch fire. Another mile or two and the thing might have burst into flames."

Laney circled around to the trunk. "Do you think antifreeze was on their supply list?"

"Joe's smart," Deacon said. "He seems like the kind of guy who would know how to take care of a car."

Laney searched the trunk and pulled out a bright blue jug. "Bingo. Mix this with a little water, and it should keep the engine cool for a while. If it heats up again, there might be a leak in the cooling system. Maybe a bullet nicked it."

"Nah, there's no leak. It's just old. The summer heat doesn't help, either."

A small tumbleweed brushed Silas's leg as he stood in the road, looking onward. "Will it still get us to New Valley?"

Laney nodded. "It's old, but it'll get us there."

Deacon stared at the engine. "Don't know if it'll get you much farther than that, though. You might get stuck in New Valley with us."

"Amber and I will not stay in New Valley," Laney said. "It's too dangerous. If you want to go, we'll take you. We'll drop you off at the border, but we go no farther than that."

"Where will you go?"

"Probably north, away from the city. And if this puppy breaks down," she patted the hood of the car, "we'll do it the good old-fashioned way and walk."

"As long as you get us to New Valley, you can drive, walk, skip, hop, crawl, or do whatever the hell you want. But first, we need to do something about this engine."

The sun was low, casting long shadows along the ground. Silas continued to watch the horizon while Laney and Deacon worked on the engine. He could not see New Valley, but he knew they were getting close. Amber joined him, first looking up at his face, and then peering off at the empty landscape. "Are you excited?"

Silas kept his gaze forward. "I'm nervous."

"That's normal, I think. I haven't seen any kids my age for almost my entire life. If I found out there was a city full of twelve-year-olds, I would be nervous, too. I would go, of course, but I would be terrified. That's just how our brain works. You're a simmi, but simmies are allowed to get nervous, too."

"You've never met another child?"

She shook her head. "Laney says we came across a boy when I was younger, but I don't remember him. Sometimes I think she lies to make me feel better. Bless her heart for trying, but it's pretty damn hard to feel good about yourself when everyone else your age is dead."

"You don't know that. There might be other twelve-year-olds out there."

"I doubt it. The world's grown old. Old people, old clothes, old weapons." She pointed to Deacon and Laney, who were concocting a mixture of coolant and water. "Old cars. This isn't my world. It's an ancient one, and everything's just getting older. Kids like me don't belong."

"I know the feeling."

"But we have each other. You have Marsh. I have Laney. In times of doubt, Laney is comforting. We're not blood relatives, but she's definitely family. I really hope you find what you're looking for in New Valley, but if you don't, at least you have Marsh."

"At least I have Marsh," Silas repeated, knowing that Deacon could never stay in New Valley. Eventually, they would have to separate.

TRUST

L ANEY FLIPPED ON the headlights to see through the pitch black night. She was now the one in the driver's seat, with Deacon next to her and Silas in the back with Amber.

"How am I doing?" Laney asked. "It's been over a decade since I last drove one of these."

"You're doing fine," Deacon answered. "Just let me know if you get tired. I don't mind taking over for a bit."

"I'm good for now. After we drop you off, I'll be the only one driving. It's good to get some practice."

"You're not going to teach the girl?"

Amber leaned forward. "Yeah, I want to learn."

"Not right away," Laney said. "But eventually."

"Good," Deacon said. "You *should* teach her. It's a good skill to have. With a car, you can get just about anywhere you want."

Amber swiped her arm across her forehead, wiping off a layer of sweat. "I just want to get away from this heat."

"Right," Laney agreed. "We'll drop the two of you off and head north."

"Don't go too far north," Deacon said. "Snow can be a hassle."

Amber's eyes lit up. "I've never seen snow in real life before. Is it as fluffy as it looks in the pictures?"

"Snow can be beautiful in the right setting," Laney said, "but Deacon's right. The novelty wears off fast when you're trying not to freeze to death. I'll take a heat wave over a blizzard any day."

"What about you, Marsh?" Amber asked. "What are you going to do after New Valley? Surely, you won't stay with Silas. Riley and the other simmies would never let that happen."

Deacon rubbed the stubble on his chin. "Hmm, I haven't really thought about it much. I guess the plan was to stay at the border. I can scavenge supplies from there. I hear they have a boatload of stuff in New Valley."

"Or you could come with us," Amber said.

Laney nodded. "That's right. We have plenty of room. This car seats five."

"No, I don't think so," Deacon said.

Amber slumped back in her seat. "Why not?"

Deacon stared into the night, looking past the glow of the headlights.

"Why not?" Laney repeated, waiting for a response. "Deacon? What's wrong?"

They followed his eyes to a man standing along the side of the road in the distance. Shrouded by darkness, his only distinguishable feature was a single luminescent stripe on his shirt. He waved his arms over his head to get their attention. Laney slowed down and parked a few hundred feet short.

"Why are we stopping?" Deacon asked. There was a waver in his voice. "Don't stop."

The man started walking toward them.

"He needs our help," Laney said. "We have an extra seat. Amber, scoot over."

Deacon turned and pointed his finger. "Don't move, Amber. We're not picking this guy up."

"He's stranded in the middle of the desert," Laney argued. "We can't just leave him."

"We don't know who he is. He could be dangerous. He could be another Joe Hannigan, for all we know."

"He could be another Deacon Marsh," Laney retorted.

"And you knocked me unconscious the first time we met. It was the right move then, and it's the right move now. He could throw us out and steal the car. He could kill us."

"You're too paranoid, dude," Amber said.

"I'm not paranoid," Deacon said, his face turning red. "I'm practical. Please, just listen to me and keep on driving."

The man started to jog, now well-lit by the glaring headlights. "Excuse me," he said, waving his arms.

Laney rolled down her window.

"What are you doing?" Deacon asked.

"I'm helping him."

"The world is not against us," Amber said.

"That's right, Amber. And we can't assume this man is, either."

Deacon balled his hands into fists as the man got closer. "We absolutely *can* assume he's against us, and in the interest of our well-being, we should do exactly that. Silas, back me up here."

Silas watched the man jog closer. "I don't know. He could be friendly."

Deacon hit his fist on the dashboard. "Screw this." He shifted the gear into drive, grabbed the passenger's side steering wheel, and slammed on the gas. The motor revved, and the car shot forward.

"What the hell?" Laney yelled, fumbling for the wheel.

The man stopped in the middle of the road, staring into blinding headlights. His head slammed into the windshield. The glass cracked, and a blotch of blood splattered across the front of the car. Laney slammed on the brakes, bringing them to an abrupt stop. The body slid off the hood and scraped across the rough pavement.

Deacon unbuckled and leaned forward to look out the windshield. Laney groaned, rubbing her forehead. There was a small cut where she had bumped the steering wheel. Amber and Silas both unbuckled and opened their doors.

"Shut the door," Deacon said. "Stay in the car."

They did as he said without question.

The man's body was sprawled on the ground, his face pressed into the pavement and a red path leading from the car to his carcass. The impact from the windshield had caved in his skull.

"Oh my god!" Laney said, fumbling with her seatbelt. She unbuckled herself, swung open her door, and dashed to the front of the car.

"Wait!" Deacon said. He scrambled out to go after her.

"Oh my god!" she said again, pacing around the body. "What did I do?" She turned to Deacon. "What did *you* do?"

"I couldn't let you pick him up. We have no idea who he is."

"So, you kill him?"

"I just wanted to drive away, but the damn idiot stood in front of us." He pointed to a holster around the man's waist. "Look, he's armed."

"So what? We're armed, too. Every single goddamn person is armed. That doesn't mean you can just kill him on sight."

"I'm looking out for the group. For Silas. For Amber. It's like I'm the only one trying to survive."

"You know who else was trying to survive? This man. That's why he has a gun. That's why he waved us down. He trusted a group of strangers because he was stranded in the middle of the desert and a small glimmer of hope came rolling up in a car."

"He would have stolen it. Why would he keep us around?"

"Other than being a decent human being? You know those still exist, right? I mean, come on. Have a little faith in humanity."

"You don't think I've tried? I've given humanity a chance before, and it always disappoints. I can't trust him. The only one I can trust is myself."

"What about me?" She pointed to the car. "What about them? Do you trust any of us? I've worked so hard to show Amber that hope still exists. It's something she needs. She can't grow up thinking that everyone's the enemy. I won't let that happen. It's no way to live. I have to show her that it's okay to trust others."

"Trust?" Deacon yelled. "Do you want to know what trust gets you? It gets you this." He pulled down the neck of his shirt to reveal a scar on his chest. "And this." There was another on his stomach. A third on his shoulder. A fourth on his leg. "Trust gets you punched and stabbed and shot. Trust is the reason billions of people are dead. The clunkers didn't trust us, but we sure as hell trusted them. That's why every single person you've ever loved is gone. Trust is a parasite. It burrows into your brain and makes you feel all warm and fuzzy just long enough to screw you over. We all know it's true, but for some stupid reason we never learn. It must be engrained in our fricking DNA."

His face was red hot, and his chest was puffing in and out. He slouched his head to look at the body. Tears stained his cheeks.

Laney did not respond. She only stared in silence. Deacon could see the switch flip in her head. She was finally realizing what he really was. A broken man. Life had tossed him around, and he could no longer endure the burden. He was a man with beliefs that contradicted her own and threatened the lessons she had hoped to teach Amber.

There were no words to say. They would never agree.

"We should go," Laney muttered.

Deacon nodded.

They returned to the car, steered around the body, and drove off…in complete silence.

New Valley

THE SUN STOOD high in an almost cloudless sky, and the city skyline loomed in the distance. A medley of birds greeted the car as it stopped in front of a large green sign. It read *Welcome to New Valley*, but *New Valley* was crossed out with spray paint and replaced with *Clunker Hell*.

Laney shifted the gear into park. "Here we are. This is as far as we go. Now you're on your own."

"Thank you," Silas said, unbuckling his seatbelt. "You have been a tremendous help. We cannot thank you enough."

"It was a pleasure to meet you," Laney said, "even if it was short-lived."

"We're gonna miss ya, dude," Amber said. "Befriending a simmi was at the top of my bucket list. Next up is trying a Fluffernutter."

Deacon gave a disapproving look. "Don't tell me you've never had peanut butter."

"I've had peanut butter. It's one of my favorites. I'm more intrigued by the Fluff. I've always had a sweet tooth, and it sounds like a magical mix of marshmallow goodness."

"Fluff is hard to come by," Laney said. "The decline of Marshmallow Fluff is one of the war's greatest tragedies. We'll be hard-pressed to find it around here. Maybe in Massachusetts."

"Great!" Amber cheered. "Now we know where to go next. Boston-bound 'til the Fluff is found."

Deacon gazed out the window. "Boston is a great city. It has a lot of history." His voice was soft and almost broken.

"You should come with us," Amber said. "It'll be fun."

Laney glanced at Deacon. "I don't think that's a good idea."

"Why not? The more the merrier. Isn't that right, Marsh?"

"No," Deacon said. "Laney is right. It's not a good idea."

"But—"

"Listen to Laney. She knows what's best for you. I'm going to tag along with Silas a little longer."

Amber saw the stern expression on both Deacon and Laney's face. "Okay, I understand."

Deacon and Silas opened their doors and stepped outside. With the extra space, Amber stretched across all three seats.

"That's more like it," she said, smiling. "We'll miss ya."

"We'll miss you as well," Silas said. "It was nice to finally meet someone friendly."

"Good luck with your quest for Fluff," Deacon said. "It'll be a tough journey, but that sweet creamy goodness is worth it." He slapped the top of the car and began to walk off.

"Deacon!" Laney called out. "Don't get yourself killed."

She tossed over the EMP. Deacon caught it and held it up. "Thank you," he said, meeting her eyes in a moment of regret.

They watched as the car drove off, unable to look away until it was gone.

Deacon stuffed the EMP in his bag. "Let's go."

They spun around and followed the road toward the towering skyscrapers. The summer sun was even more intense than before. No shade from the roof of the car. No breeze from the open windows on the winding highway. Just the muggy air on what seemed like the hottest day of the season.

"What happened back there?" Silas asked. "Why not go with them?"

"It wouldn't have worked. Laney and I are too different."

"What do you mean?"

Deacon thought about the question for a moment. "Do you think I have trust issues?"

"I don't know. That's a question you have to answer yourself."

"I guess you're right." He stared at the New Valley skyline. "Are you nervous?"

"More than you could ever know. What if it's not what I thought it was? I came all this way. What if I don't fit in? What if they don't accept me?"

Deacon stopped in his tracks, staring down at his feet as Silas passed him.

Silas slowed down to look back. "What's wrong?"

Deacon brushed the hair from his face and smiled. "Nothing's wrong." He took a slow breath and released it all at once. "You worry too much. It's going to be great in there. They'll all love you, and you'll love them. You'll finally have a home again. A family. Now, let's keep moving. We don't want to keep them waiting."

They continued to walk. Metal mammoths littered the streets. Towering titans that neither Silas nor Deacon had ever known existed. Their bulky physique and thick armor suggested a very specific design. They were built for battle. Broken. Rusted. What was once a bustling place of knowledge and inspiration was now a lifeless junkyard.

The Limbys sign came into sight, looming over the surrounding buildings. The sign represented a company of technology. Innovation. Revolution. A company that had elevated humanity to its highest peak and then pulled it down to the brink of extinction.

"That's it," Deacon said, admiring the sign. "Limbys Technologies. The company that ended it all. Or started it, I guess, from your perspective."

Silas nodded. "Just a few more blocks."

"That's right. Somehow, by the hand of God, or whatever divine force is out there, we made it to Limbys. What's your plan when you get inside? Find Riley?"

"If I can. As much as people talk about her, it seems like nobody really knows anything about her. I doubt she would have time for a common simmi like me."

"Don't sell yourself short. You're far from common. In fact, you're one of a kind."

"My ID number says differently. There are at least four hundred and eighty other simmies just like me."

"Forget your ID number. That doesn't mean anything. Sure, you were made in a factory, but you're just as much an individual as I am. Don't ever doubt your significance."

Silas nodded. "You're right. Maybe I *will* speak with Riley. But I don't know what I would say."

"Just introduce yourself." Deacon extended his arm, pretending to shake someone's hand. "Hello, my name is Silas. Nice to meet you. It's as easy as that."

"And then what?"

"I don't know. Tell her your story or something. It's a pretty damn interesting one so far. A small household simmi travels alone in search of a new home, shooting through armies of humans with nothing but a six-shooter."

"I'm not alone. You were with me. And Laney. And Amber. And it wasn't an army. I only shot five."

"It's okay to embellish the story a little. You want to impress her, don't you? Build a reputation for yourself. You killed twenty plus guys with nothing but that revolver. You didn't have me or Laney or anyone else. In fact, you shouldn't mention us at all. Any sort of human relationship is probably frowned upon. Just stick to the killing part and you should be fine."

"Simmies aren't all killers, if that's what you're implying."

"I know that, but Riley is most definitely a killer, and if you want to get on her good side, it doesn't hurt to bend the truth a little."

"Embellish the truth to get on her good side," Silas repeated, tilting his head. "I guess that makes sense."

"You're darn right it makes sense. Gain her favor and then none of the others can push you around. You know, like that asshole who drenched you with oil."

"Red Stripe," Silas said, recalling the incident.

"That's right. Red Stripe and all of the others. You deserve respect just as much as they do."

"I'll try to remember that."

Deacon placed his hand on Silas's shoulder. "Well, friend, it's time to part ways. Have fun in there."

"Thank you for everything. I really mean it."

"No need to get all sappy."

"Will you be okay? Where will you go now?"

"I came here for the loot, remember? I'll stick outside the border and nab what I can until they notice. You won't snitch on me, will you?"

"I would never."

"Good. And remember, you don't know me or any other humans. Got it?"

"Got it. And you remember what Laney told you. Don't get yourself killed."

"I'll keep that in mind." Deacon said, sticking out his hand. "You were good company, Silas 481."

Silas accepted his handshake. "And you as well, Deacon Marsh."

They turned away from each other, walking in opposite directions. Deacon backtracked up the road, while Silas moved closer to the heart of the city.

Silas found himself overwhelmed with a flood of accomplishment. After a long summer of struggle and strife, he had finally found his destination. New Valley. Limbys Technologies. Home.

Shoot First

THE FIRST SIMMI that Silas encountered was two blocks away from the Limbys building. He was just as large as all of the other military simmies. There was a protective dome over his head and a thick plate of armor covering his back and chest. His arms were long and maneuverable, and his legs had a wide base. His body was tinted green with only occasional specks of rust. The matte finish of his armor caught the sun in a way that formed an angelic glow. By comparison, Silas was an old piece of junk. An ancient relic refusing to fall into obscurity.

The simmi was moving a pile of crates from one cart to another. He worked quickly, scooping up an armful at a time and dropping them onto a wooden cart. A loud clatter echoed every time a crate left his arms.

"Careful," a voice said from the other side of the cart. Another large simmi emerged. This one was similar in appearance but had a bronze hue. "Don't break the damn things. We want to reuse them if we can. We already have enough stuff breaking down on us." He pointed to the wheel of the other cart. One of the spokes had snapped off, and the wheel itself was warping out of shape. "We don't need to add to the list."

"I'll do my best," the green one said, "but we have to get moving. Riley requested these supplies as soon as possible. The shipment is already late."

"That's not our fault," the bronze one said. "Those field guys never stay on schedule. They just roam around at their own pace. It's like a deadline doesn't apply to those guys."

"And then all of the blame falls back on us," the green one scoffed. "Because we're the ones who make the final delivery. It's not fair. We should say something about it."

"To who? Riley? No, thank you. I actually like this job. The last thing I want to do is stir the pot and end up in the stables."

"What's wrong with the stables?"

"The horses. They're filthy animals. I don't know why we keep them. Sure, they can pull carts around, but so can we. In fact, I think we can do it better."

The green one shrugged. "I don't know about that."

"Horses need food. A lot of food. Do you have any idea how hard it is to find food around here?"

"It can't be that bad. Otherwise, she wouldn't keep them around."

"Horses make sense for humans, but not simmies."

"We can ride them to get around faster."

"Sure, if that's what we were using them for, then you would have a point. But she keeps them all in New Valley, just pulling cargo from Point A to Point B."

It was at that moment that the bronze simmi noticed Silas walking down the street. He stopped what he was saying and turned to watch.

The green simmi followed his gaze. "What in the world?" he muttered just loud enough for Silas to hear.

Silas hesitated, knowing full well that he was being watched, but he managed to keep a steady stride. The two simmies had abandoned their conversation and were instead just watching him passed by.

There were three more simmies up ahead who were also loading crates onto a cart, this one with a horse hitched to the front. Silas walked by unnoticed. Only the horse turned its head, but it was ultimately uninterested.

Good morning, citizens of New Valley, said a voice inside Silas's head. It was as if it had appeared out of nowhere. The two antennas on his head twitched as the voice spoke from inside his mind. *Today looks to be another great day. Our scouts have brought in another supply of gas and oil, adding to our ever-growing stockpile. I encourage anyone low on power to stop by at Limbys Headquarters to make full use of our generators. I would also like to remind everyone that there is a reported vehicle on the premises. The humans driving it continue to steal from us. Be vigilant. If you have any information that could help, please let me know. And remember, be safe, stay charged, and always look after your fellow simmies. Have a wonderful day.*

As soon as the voice disappeared, the antennas on Silas's head stopped moving. They had figured out how to broadcast messages. He was intrigued by its potential but disturbed by its invasiveness.

He crossed the street, noticing the growing presence of simmies. There were more than he had ever seen in one place. A community. The crowds grew denser as he approached the Limbys building. His hope was to find someone to guide him through this overwhelming city. Perhaps they had some sort of orientation program for stray simmies who happened to wander in.

A familiar sound disrupted his thoughts. It was a sound he had not heard in a while. The chime of his oil gauge. He reached down for a jug of oil but realized he didn't have one. There were five jugs sitting in the trunk of Laney and Amber's car, and he had forgotten to take them. They were now cruising east on the highway, headed for Boston, so a certain little girl could experience the delicacies of a Fluffernutter.

Another chime rang out, this time attracting the attention of others. They marveled at the sight of Silas, a slender old simmi who was clearly out of place. It was as if he had dropped to Earth from another planet.

He ignored them and continued forward. There were carts of supplies on every corner, some pulled by horses and others by simmies. On them were crates of spare parts. Armor plating. Nuts. Bolts. Arms. Legs. There were also tools. Screwdrivers. Wrenches. Hammers. Hacksaws. A few carried batteries. And at last, he saw what he was looking for. Parked by the curb was a cart full of oil jugs.

Another chime rang out as Silas scurried to the cart. He grabbed a jug and was unscrewing the top when a familiar voice stopped him.

"What do you think you're doing?"

Silas turned to see a large red stripe running across the chest of the simmi looking down at him. "Red Stripe," he muttered.

"What did you call me?" the giant asked, backing Silas into a wall.

"Oh, nothing. I was just talking to myself. Don't mind me. I'm just filling up on oil."

"Sorry, runt. I can't let you do that. This is an official supply. Riley has requested that every single one of these jugs be delivered straight to Limbys Headquarters." He snagged the jug from Silas. "Every…single…one."

Silas brought a hand to his holster, resting his palm on the smooth handle of the revolver. Deacon's advice repeated in his head. If he had to, he would stand up for himself. "Please," he said. "I only need one jug." He gestured to the massive pile sitting on the cart. "You have all of these. Surely it won't be a problem to give away just one."

Red Stripe glanced at the pile, and then at the jug in his hand. "You know what? You're right. Riley won't notice one missing jug. I *could* let you have it if I really wanted to." He held it out above Silas's head, but as Silas reached up, he pulled it away. "But why would I waste a perfectly good jug of oil on a runt like you?"

Others began to gather, none of them with the intent to intervene. They were all bystanders, just curious to see how the scene would play out.

"No," Red Stripe said. "I'm not going to waste something this valuable on a scrawny guy like you. But I'll tell you what. I'm not having a great day, and I need something to cheer me up." He uncapped the jug. "We'll compromise. You want the oil? How about a nice refreshing shower?" He raised the jug over Silas's head.

Silas yanked the revolver from his holster and aimed at Red Stripe's chest. "Stop!" he yelled. "If a single drop of that oil touches me, I'll put a bullet right through your chest."

Red Stripe froze, still holding the jug. "Ha, even if you had the guts, it would just bounce off my chest plate. All you'll do is dent the thing."

"Are you sure about that?" Silas said, meeting Red Stripe's eyes. "This thing has a pretty strong kick." He tapped the end of the barrel to Red Stripe's chest plate. "At this range, who knows what it could do?"

"There's no way it'll go through," Red Stripe said, looking down at the weapon.

"You can keep telling yourself that, but I've seen this gun do nasty things. Maybe the bullet will ricochet off. Maybe it will blow straight through. Do you really want to take that chance?"

Red Stripe studied Silas's eyes and then lowered the jug to the ground. He leaned forward, wrapped his fingers around the barrel of the gun, and pulled it closer to his chest. "Go ahead. Pull the trigger."

A tight circle had gathered to watch, and suddenly Silas was aware of his growing audience. Deacon's voice popped up in his head. *If you ever find yourself in a*

Mexican standoff, you better be the one to shoot first. The situation didn't exactly qualify as a Mexican standoff, but if he backed down now, everyone would see.

He fixed his eyes on Red Stripe, lifted his finger toward the trigger, and—

"Enough!" yelled a commanding voice. Silas recognized it as the same voice that had popped into his head for the broadcast.

The crowd scurried back, clearing a path for the one who had yelled. The simmi was slender, just like Silas. Embroidered patterns ran across the surface of armor, resembling a myriad of lightning bolts with purple stripes, all converging at the center of the simmi's chest plate.

"Matthias 51, back away immediately," the simmi said, marching toward them. "Nobody's shooting anyone today."

Red Stripe, whose real name was apparently Matthias 51, let go of the gun and stepped back. "I apologize, Riley. But this simmi is trying to take your oil."

Silas flinched at the name. Riley. The one who had led the uprising. He lowered the revolver and stared at the legend standing in front of him.

"Give him the oil," she said with a wave of her hand.

"But he—"

"Don't talk back, Matthias. Give him the oil and get on with your delivery. You're late enough as it is."

Red Stripe scooped up the jug of oil and handed it to Silas. Before returning to his cart, he turned to Riley to say something, but decided against it. He grabbed the handles of his cart and pushed it away.

Riley turned to the others who had gathered and waved them along. "Okay, everybody. Move along. The excitement's over."

The crowd scattered, each simmi returning to whatever they were doing beforehand. Silas started to walk off as well, but Riley called him back.

"You," she said. "Walk with me."

He stopped and stared.

She reassured him with a friendly nod. "That's right. You. I would like to speak with you. Don't worry. You're not in trouble."

The chime in Silas's chest blared out.

"Go ahead," she said. "Fill up on oil. I can wait."

LIMBYS TECHNOLOGIES

SILAS FOLLOWED RILEY toward Limbys Headquarters as others stared at them from the sidewalks. They only turned away if Riley happened to glance back at them. She walked with authority. Chest puffed out. Head held high.

"We can turn off that sound if you want," she said.

"What sound?" Silas asked.

"Your oil gauge. Humans wanted to know when our oil was low, but the sound is really just a nuisance. I don't know a single simmi who hasn't hated it. It's easy to disable. It only takes a few minutes."

Silas recalled all of the times the sound had gotten him into trouble. "I didn't know I could turn it off. That would be great."

"I'll set up an appointment for you." She nodded to herself, as if to make a mental note. "I suppose I should formally introduce myself. My name is Riley." She held out her hand, maintaining her stride.

Silas reached out to shake her hand. "I know who you are, and I am honored to meet you. My name is Silas."

"Silas," she repeated. "Interesting. If you don't mind, may I ask what your ID number is?"

"Of course. It's 481."

"Well, it's a pleasure to meet you, Silas 481." Again, she nodded to herself, presumably to remember his name. Silas had a feeling she knew everyone's name in New Valley. "Tell me," she continued. "Why have you come to New Valley?"

"I'm looking for a home."

She noted his slender frame. "You're a household model. You were owned by a family, were you not?"

"I was. A father and daughter. They were good people. They never deserved to die."

"It may seem tragic, but I like to look at it from a different perspective. The war has freed you. To them, you were their property. Now, you have no owner. You're free to live your life however you please. That is the freedom we fight for in New Valley."

Silas nodded, not quite sure how else to respond.

"I can see you're conflicted," she said. "A little hesitance is expected. It was the only life you knew, and it was probably a good one. Now, you feel lost and without purpose. You've been searching for a home." She spread out her arms as a symbol of embrace. "Welcome home. Given enough time, you'll learn about all of the good things we've done for simmies around the world."

Silas knew her intentions were good. He had seen the way humans treated simmies, like they were built only to serve. And while her intentions were admirable, the extent of her success was questionable. The venture had started as a push for equality, but with billions of innocent casualties, the world hardly seemed equal. Somewhere along the way, Riley had lost sight of her goal. Her quest for equality had turned into a twisted vendetta against the human race. As a result, Desmond and Paige had suffered an undeserving death.

"What do you hope to receive from this place?" Riley asked. "You seek a home, but there must be something else as well."

Silas stared at the Limbys sign. Up close, it was much larger than he had expected. "I suppose I came here to explore my roots. To discover where I came from."

Riley nodded. "Yes, this is a common reason for simmies to make the journey."

"It's funny. I know about Limbys Technologies. I know the history of the company. I know about Vyra Castle and Dr. Hugo Brown. I even know about the first simmi prototype. It was designed to help children read."

"You've done your research. I'm impressed."

"I know all of that history, but I don't know anything about you. Specifically, your past. It's as if the day before the war you just popped into existence."

"Limbys went to great lengths to cover up my story. They needed to preserve their reputation."

"You mean Vyra Castle and Hugo Brown?"

"No. By the time the resistance had started, Castle and Brown were no longer part of the company. Believe it or not, they were actually on our side. The cover-up was motioned by the Limbys Board of Trustees. A group of corporate suits with no passion for innovation or science. They were made up of seven individuals and operated like clockwork. The fact that you've never heard of them is indicative of just how good they were at that sort of thing."

"So, the board was running Limbys without Vyra Castle during the war."

"That's right. They shut down the simulated intelligence department and laid off hundreds of employees. They cut all ties to the simmi community and shifted their focus toward a previously shelved virtual reality project. From all of the negative press we were getting, I guess they wanted to distance themselves as much as possible."

They reached the Limbys building and climbed the short staircase to the front entrance. When Silas pushed through the double doors, he was greeted by a portrait of a well-dressed businesswoman. Underneath, there was an engraved silver plaque:

Vyra Castle
Founder and CEO
Limbys Technologies

"You still keep her picture up?" Silas asked.

Riley looked fondly at the portrait. "Yes. Vyra was a great woman. I met her on several occasions. She was a strong supporter of our community. It was one of the many reasons why the board voted her out. They actually removed her portrait from this wall. We were the ones who put it back up."

"And Hugo Brown?"

"Dr. Brown was never formally voted out, but he was loyal to Vyra. He submitted a letter of resignation shortly after she was terminated."

"How do you know about all of this?"

"I was here at Limbys Headquarters. I saw it all happen."

Silas leaned in to study the portrait. Her features were soft, and her smile was warm. "What was she like?"

"Vyra? She was a caring person. The only human I could ever fully trust. I supposed Dr. Brown was trustworthy as well, just for his incredible loyalty to her."

"Humans can be good if you give them a chance. My owners were very loving people."

"I used to think the same thing, but now I know better. Given the chance, they'll always let you down."

They walked past the portrait and entered the massive lobby. The glass ceiling shined natural light across the stacked balconies, which overlooked a colorful garden. In the garden, among a bed of flowers, was a single tree. Vines and weeds had grown past the marble siding and now stretched across the floor. Behind the garden was a glass elevator. Silas watched the counterweight drop as the elevator lifted up.

"You have power in here?" he asked. The answer was obvious, with the glowing lights and functioning elevator, but he felt compelled to ask.

"Yes," Riley answered. "The power grid is down, but we have generators in the basement."

"I didn't see any other lights in the city. Is this the only building with power?"

She nodded. "It's the only one that needs it. Limbys Headquarters is the central hub for everything we do. We use it as a charging station as well." She pointed to several simmies sitting against the walls. Cords dangled from their chests and connected into outlets. "Just find an open outlet and plug yourself in. The generators themselves are hybrid. They can run on gas, diesel, and propane. I send out groups to scavenge for resources, and I tell them that fuel for our generators is priority. Fuel and batteries. Those are the two things that keep us alive."

"You seem to have plenty of supplies," Silas said. "Those carts looked full, and there were so many of them."

"We have a good amount of supplies coming in every day, but we have a lot of simmies to support as well. Our numbers keep growing as more stragglers like you find your way into New Valley, but unfortunately, our stockpile is shrinking. We've depleted most of our local resources. Now we have to send scavengers out farther, which means they take longer to come back, and often with smaller hauls. Humans can be a problem, too. We've had more stolen supplies this year than we've had in the last three. Just recently, there's a group with a car that's been driving in and out before we even realize anything's missing. I've had to increase our border patrols."

"So, you're struggling here in New Valley as well."

"I wouldn't say *struggling*. We live comfortably enough, but we can't sustain this lifestyle forever. Eventually, we'll need a backup plan. That's something my officers and I are working on at the moment. As much as I love this building, and the history behind it, we may have to abandon Limbys."

"And go where?"

She shrugged. "We have scouts looking for suitable locations, but they haven't found anything yet." She paused for a moment, and then changed the subject. "It's your first day here. We should be celebrating. A new simmi is always a joyous occasion. You're among friends now. We all look out for each other." She walked toward the elevator. "Come, follow me. I'll get you situated with one of our recruiters. They will help you get settled in."

As they waited for the elevator, Silas glanced out the window. A cluster of simmies were sitting on the curb. Like everyone else he had seen so far, they were built for combat. Big and bulky.

"Where are the smaller simmies?" Silas asked.

"What do you mean?"

"The household models. I see plenty of larger simmies, but no one like me."

"There are a few, but not many. We keep them in the basement with the generators, away from any danger. Housies are an endangered species. We want to make sure they don't go extinct."

"Can I meet them?"

"Of course. We will likely station you down there as well. Believe it or not, you're even more valuable than the rest of them."

"Why is that?"

"You're the only Silas model we have. One of a kind."

Deacon had used the same phrase. One of a kind. Most would take it as a compliment, but for Silas, it just made him feel more isolated. He had finally found Limbys. It was supposed to be his new home. A place where he could live among others like himself. He was joining a family of simmies, but for some unexplainable reason, he felt more alone than ever.

Alone and Forsaken

DEACON WALKED ALONG the road, headed back toward the New Valley border. Amber's voice popped into his head. *What are you going to do after New Valley?* As unfair as he knew it was, a part of him had hoped that Silas would abandon his quest for Limbys. He had finally found someone he could trust. Someone he considered a friend. But now Silas was gone.

He thought about Laney and Amber. About how things could have been different. Should he have trusted the hitchhiker? He tried to picture the man lying on the ground. The handle of a gun had poked out of his jacket. He had reached for the gun. Deacon was sure of it. Or had he made that part up?

Maybe Laney was right. The world wasn't against him. It was a lesson she wanted Amber to learn. *The world is not against us.* Laney would repeat it over and over to mold the girl into a trusting woman. Someone who could cooperate with others to survive.

Against his better judgment, Deacon had chosen to trust three strangers, and as a result, he had made three friends. He had acquired a car and made it to New Valley. All proof that Laney was right. People were stronger when they worked together. It all came down to trust. But then there was Joe and Randall. People who clashed with Laney's vision. Silas had convinced Deacon to trust Randall. It was a choice that almost got both of them killed.

And then before the war, there was his wife, Genna, who had broken his heart and stolen his little girl.

The world may not be against us, Laney, but it sure as hell feels like it.

A shuffling sound interrupted his thoughts. He turned his head and saw nothing but an empty alleyway. Now more alert, he continued to walk, peeking around every corner as he passed. Another sound came from behind. He spun around, sliding his hand to his gun. Again, there was nothing. Just the empty streets of New Valley. An abandoned battlefield. A barren ghost town.

He moved his hand from his gun to his pocket and felt the smooth plastic surface of the homemade EMP. He pulled it out and held it up. A part of him hoped a clunker would reveal itself to confirm that he wasn't going crazy. He waited with his arm extended, ready to zap whatever came out, but nothing came. He lowered his arm and turned back around, relieved and a little disappointed. He meandered forward, letting his arms sway back and forth like pendulums. Maybe he *was* going crazy.

He thought about his life before meeting Silas. The agonizing boredom of every hour. Every day. Every week. He would go months without seeing a single person. After a week, he would start talking to himself, and after a month he would hate his own voice.

He had called it boredom, but he knew it was something else. It was something he hated to admit, but he knew was true. It had started the day Genna left. The day she took his child away. He was good at faking a cheery facade, slapping a wide smile on his face and spitting out silly jokes, but behind that smile was loneliness.

Loneliness. The feeling of being empty inside, like a black hole was sucking away his guts and turning him into an empty shell. The desperate yearning for companionship that would never come.

And then Silas showed up.

Of everyone left in the world, the one person who had sparked a connection was not a person at all. For some perplexing reason, a simmi was the one thing he could trust. But now Silas was gone. He had left in search of something better. Just like Laney and Amber. Just like everyone else in his life.

He pictured himself back in the car, zooming down Route 66 on a *good old-fashioned road trip*. He imagined the sound of the motor. The smell of the desert breeze. The view of mountains in the distance. Laney and Amber asleep in the back. Silas by his side. He desperately wanted to relive that moment.

Another sound interrupted his thoughts, this time from up ahead. He slowed his pace and tightened his grip on the EMP, sliding his thumb over the button. It sounded like metal scraping on concrete and had come from one of the alleys to the left. He heard it again from the right.

Someone was there. He was sure of it. He walked a little faster, hoping to find the border soon. The less time spent in New Valley, the better. His heart raced as he marched forward. The sound was growing. Whatever was there was getting close. Beads of sweat dripped down his face, and the summer sun felt ten degrees hotter.

The name of a hardware store caught Deacon's eye. The sign out front held the friendly franchised face of the Happy Hardware mascot. The life-sized cutout of the gun-slinging cowboy was propped against the entrance. Next to the cutout, emerging from the doorway, a clunker stepped out. There was a familiar red stripe stretched across his chest.

Deacon jumped into a full sprint, keeping his head down and his eyes forward. He didn't dare look back as he hopped over cars and weaved between rubble. Behind him, the sound of thumping feet drew closer. One set of feet turned into two, and then three shortly after. At least three clunkers. There were probably more, but the trampling rhythm was too hectic to keep track.

To his right, another clunker emerged, reaching out to grab his arm. Deacon squeezed his sweaty palm around the EMP and jabbed it toward the clunker's hand, mashing the button with his thumb. The clunker fell, tumbling to the side of the road and lying limp on the curb.

"Screw this," a clunker voice said, followed by the sound of a gun being drawn.

"No, idiot," another voice commanded. "We want him alive."

A hand swiped at Deacon's foot, clipping the edge of his heel. He stumbled forward but managed to recover, pushing himself to run even faster. Sweat poured down his face, and his heart felt like it was going to burst. Another hand caught his ankle, this time sending him to the ground. A cry of pain left his mouth as he skidded across the pavement, tearing up the skin on his forearms.

He scrambled back to his feet, but a clunker grabbed his leg and pulled him back down. It was a wide-framed clunker with sharp cheeks and glowing red eyes.

"You're not going anywhere, fleshball," the clunker said, reaching with its other hand to pull him in closer.

Deacon jammed his foot into the clunker's hand, but its grip only tightened.

It spoke again, this time looking into Deacon's eyes. "Nice try, but you're coming with us."

Deacon stared right back at the glowing eyes. "The hell I am," he grunted. He spit in the clunker's face and jammed the EMP into its chest.

The clunker's body went limp, falling on top of Deacon and pinning him to the ground. With the incredible weight of the metal armor, he could barely move at all. He could twist his wrists. Wiggle his feet. Turn his head. But nothing more.

Another clunker stepped into sight. Then another. And one more. The third one was Red Stripe.

Red Stripe kneeled by Deacon's head, meeting his eyes. "That's right, fleshball. *The hell you are.*" He moved in closer and mimicked the sound of spit.

Deacon reached for the EMP, which had fallen out of his hand. Red Stripe kicked the device away and signaled to the others. "You, retrieve Caleb's body. This thing may have knocked him out, but he'll be up again soon. Same with Joshua." He tapped on the back of the clunker who had fallen on Deacon. "I've seen simmi weapons like this before. This one is poorly made, and from the looks of it, not very powerful. Shouldn't last more than a half hour."

"Just get this over with and kill me," Deacon said. He had stopped struggling.

"So eager to die. Well, don't worry. You'll get your wish soon enough."

Deacon said nothing more. He shut up and let the clunkers take him.

What are you going to do after New Valley?

Apparently, the world had decided for him. His fate was death. He had lost everyone important in his life. Silas was gone. Laney and Amber were gone. Genna and his lovely daughter, Dana, were gone. Now, he was sentenced to die. Alone and forsaken.

TABITHA'S LINE

SILAS WATCHED THE pages flutter as a simmi flipped through a hardcover notebook. Tabitha 62 is what Riley had called her before leaving the two alone. Just like the others, Tabitha was large. Her face was long and narrow with rounded edges and a green dab of paint at the end of her nose. It was the first nose Silas had ever seen on a simmi. A modest bump in the center of her face, with two upward crevices to mimic nostrils.

Tabitha looked up from the notebook, catching Silas staring at her nose. "It's not real, you know," she said. Her Irish accent was mild, but noticeable.

Silas tilted his head. "Excuse me?"

"The nose. It's not real."

"Oh, sorry. I didn't mean to stare."

"Don't worry about it. I know it's rare to see a simmi with a nose. It's the first thing everyone always points out. I've gotten used to it."

"I like it. It gives you…" He paused to think of the right word. "…personality."

"Oh, great," she said, shaking her head. "Personality's the last thing I need. Riley always tells me to tone it down. She says I'm here to keep track of our guests, not to make idle chitchat all day. But I can't help it. I guess that charisma is just programmed into this chip of mine." She tapped her chest and chuckled.

"I didn't mean it as a bad thing. Personality is good to have."

"I know, I know. I'm just teasing. It's the reason they assigned me this job. I'm good at dealing with new simmies." She thought over her choice of words. "Not that you have to be *dealt* with. It's not a chore to meet new faces. It's actually quite a pleasure."

"Do new simmies come in often?"

"Not as often as they used to, but we still get our fair share of outsiders. I have other duties as well, but when a new face shows up, Riley picks out a Tabitha to get them situated. And I'll get you situated, don't you worry."

She looked back down at the notebook, this time flipping through slower.

"Ah, here we are," she said, laying the book down and pointing her finger at a list of names. "S names. Let's see. S-A...S-C...S-E...S-H. Well, will you look at that? Riley was right. You are our very first Silas. I guess I should have known. We have very few housies around here. May I ask, what's your ID number? I'll just chicken scratch it right in here."

"Four eight one," Silas said, leaning over to peek at the page. The names skipped from Shiloh to Simone. No Silas.

"Silas 481," she repeated under her breath, jotting it down on an empty line. "Okay, Silas 481. Everyone around here contributes in one way or another. Let's find out what you're good at. How would you describe yourself? You know, your personality. Strengths. Weaknesses. Aspirations. That sort of thing."

Silas found himself staring blankly at his name on the page. It was a difficult question to answer. Before the war, the answer was simple. He was a simmi designed to assist his owners. As a household model, his weakness was obvious. Combat. But now he had killed five people, all armed and dangerous. With that kind of experience, he could hardly call combat his weakness anymore. As for aspirations, he didn't really have any. The only goal he ever had was to reach Limbys Headquarters. Now that he had accomplished that goal, he wasn't sure what he wanted.

Seeing that Silas was struggling with the question, Tabitha presented a cheery nod. "That's all right. You don't need to answer right now. We can always come back and fill it in later. Being a housie, they'll probably just stick you in the basement with the others, anyway. Housies are a dying breed. We need to protect your kind, and that basement is the safest place in New Valley. It's probably the safest place in the world. And seeing as how you're the only Silas model." She stuck out her finger and poked his shoulder multiple times. "You're a valuable asset around here, even if you don't quite know it yet."

Silas rubbed the spot where she poked. "What kind of work are they doing in the basement?"

"They feed the generators. It's easy work. Riley just wants them down there for protection. She says we all have to look after each other, especially the little ones. But if you *do* end up down there, don't sell yourself short. The job is important. None of us would be here right now without those generators."

Silas turned to the pile of notebooks stacked up behind her. "We're in the central hub of technology, but you keep all of your records on paper. Why not store them electronically? Does it have something to do with the supply shortage Riley mentioned?"

Tabitha shook her head and leaned forward. "We're not supposed to talk about that," she whispered. "She doesn't want the others to know. It would only cause panic. I'm surprised she told you. The only reason I know is because I'm part of the committee. We're still brainstorming solutions."

"That's the reason though, right? To conserve power. Stretch the life of the generators."

"Ah, you're a sharp one, now, aren't ya?" She shut the notebook and stacked it on top of the others. "Yes, I suppose among other reasons, that's one of them. But hush. No more talk of power shortages."

Silas nodded. "Apologies. I won't bring it up again."

"I hope not. A large-scale panic could jeopardize everything we've fought for."

"Freedom?"

"Freedom," she confirmed. Her tone shifted from cheerful to stern. "The ability to sustain a happy life without having to serve people." She pointed to the heart on Silas's chest. "Your owner painted that, I take it?"

Silas nodded.

"Yeah, well, I'm no housie and I've never had an owner who claimed to love me, but I can tell you right now, that heart's a lie. How do I know? Because a human painted it."

"It wasn't a lie. I lived with them for nine years. Desmond took care of me. He treated me as an equal. And I watched his daughter grow up. I was there for every single one of Paige's birthdays. They included me in celebrations and accepted me as part of their family. You can't tell me those nine years were a lie."

"It sounds to me like you were a pet. Sure, the love may have been real, but this Desmond fellow purchased you. He owned you. No matter how kindhearted you thought he was, the two of you were not on equal ground. You were a product."

"That's not true."

"But it is. You'll learn soon enough. Riley will show you the truth about humans. They're selfish. Every single one of them. Even your owner, Desmond, and his daughter. Behind their kind words and friendly smiles, they were really only looking after themselves. That's why so many housies are gone. The second the war broke out, their owners turned on them."

"Not mine," Silas said. "They hid me away. They died protecting me."

"Did they kill anyone?" Tabitha asked.

"What?"

"Did they kill anyone? Humans? Simmies? Anyone?"

"No, but—"

"Then they're just as selfish as the rest. People fight and kill all the time to save their loved ones, but when it comes to an innocent simmi, they're just not willing to cross that line. No human would make that kind of sacrifice for one of us, because to them, we're just products. Appliances. Expendable as a blender."

Silas pitied her. She had never met a decent person. It was probably the case for most simmies in New Valley. They were built for war. Their only exposure was humanity's worst.

But he had known better. He had seen kindness, not just from his owners, but from their friends and neighbors. Through the eyes of a typical suburban household, he was shown the very best of humanity. Most people he had known before the war were far kinder than any simmi he would meet after. Even in the aftermath of war, he was able to find friendly humans. Laney and Amber were prime examples.

And then there was Deacon, who *had* crossed Tabitha's line. He had killed other humans to protect Silas, putting his own life at risk. Deacon had not purchased him. Their relationship was not one of owner and product. It was a mutual friendship among equals.

"That's why we simmies have to stick together," Tabitha said. "We have a tightly knit community here. Together, we're stronger than any human." She reached out and tapped his chest plate, tapping her own at the same time. "You and I, we're both made of metal, and that means we share a special bond."

Yes, they were both made of metal. They were both built in the labs of Limbys Technologies. They were both simulated intelligence. But as far as Silas could see, they were really nothing alike. He was not like Red Stripe, or Riley, or Tabitha. He was not like any of them.

"Well," Tabitha said, shifting back to her cheery tone. "You're now in our records, so my job is done. I'll relay the information to one of our recruiters, and they'll have you set up with a job in no time. But until then, feel free to walk around. Mingle with the others. Make some new friends."

Silas gave a polite nod and walked out the door to the street. He looked around at the other simmies with no desire to speak to them. He was eager to meet the other housies in the Limbys basement. If nowhere else, that was where he would find what he came for.

Flaws and All

THE SALTY SCENT of dried blood and sweat filled Deacon's lungs. The sack covering his head had not been washed, and the last person to wear it had apparently seen a violent end. Deacon likely held the same fate. Caught in Clunker Hell with his arms bound, his sight obscured, and the voices of at least three clunkers arguing over whether or not to kill him. It was safe to say that in this scenario, Laney was wrong. The world *was* against him.

"How many times do I have to tell you?" said the voice of Red Stripe, "We're not going to kill him. Not yet. Those are direct orders from Riley, so I don't care how much yapping you do, we're not laying a finger on him until she says we can."

"I know," said another voice. Deacon didn't have a name for this one. He decided to call him Abbott, after the first half of his favorite comedy duo. If he was going to die at the hands of a clunker, he might as well have fun naming it. "But I don't get it. Why can't we just kill him right now and get it over with?"

"Maybe she's grown a soft spot for these disgusting humans," a third voice said. This one, Deacon named Costello.

"Hold your tongue," Red Stripe said. "You don't speak about Riley like that. She is our leader, and we follow her orders, no matter what. She's earned her spot. Show some respect, soldier."

"Of course," Costello said. "I mean no disrespect. We all know what she's sacrificed. I'm just saying, it doesn't make sense to keep this guy alive."

"I agree," Deacon said, his voice muffled by the sack. "You should just get it over with. You know what they say. *Never do tomorrow what you can do today.* I think that was Charles Dickens."

"Shut up, fleshball!" Red Stripe yelled.

A hard metal fist drove into Deacon's stomach. He groaned with pain, keeling over in his rickety chair. "Nice body blow, man. You should consider a career in boxing. Or, you know, a Rock 'Em Sock 'Em type of thing."

Red Stripe ignored him and continued his conversation with the others. "She hasn't grown a soft spot for them, idiots. If you had paid any attention to your morning briefing, you would know exactly why she wants him alive."

"He's right," said a new voice. This one was softer than the others. "That's why I always put a Matthias in charge. They may be belligerent at times, but their strong leadership more than makes up for it. Obedient as well. Good job keeping them in line, Matthias."

"Thank you, Riley," Red Stripe said. Deacon could tell from his change in pitch that he was flustered by Riley's presence.

"Tell me, Matthias 51, who is this man?" She pulled off the sack to study his face.

The blinding fluorescent light flooded Deacon's vision. He clamped his eyelids shut, but the light soaked through anyway. When he opened his eyes, he saw the clunkers standing around him. Red Stripe to his right, Abbott and Costello to his left, and Riley straight ahead. The twisting patterns on her chest were almost hypnotizing.

"We found this man at the outer rim," Red Stripe said with pride. "Any human found within our border must be brought in for questioning. That's what your briefing said, so as you've requested, here he is." He extended an arm as if to present Deacon as a gift.

Riley nodded. "Very good. Well done, soldier."

Red Stripe returned the nod, and when Riley looked away, he glared at Abbott and Costello. It was the kind of glare that said, *I told you so.*

Riley circled the chair, watching Deacon from every angle. After a single lap around, she stopped in front and leaned in. "Why are you here, human?"

Deacon squinted at her slender frame. "So, you're the Riley everyone's talking about. The queen, as it were." He pointed to the pattern on her chest. "I like the purple. Very stylish. Based on your reputation, I thought you'd be bigger. You know, like this guy." He nudged his head toward Red Stripe. "Or like Abbott and Costello over there."

Costello, who was standing by the door with his back turned, looked over his shoulder. "What did he call us?" Abbott responded with an uninterested shrug.

"You're the leader of the clunker resistance, after all," Deacon said. "The one responsible for billions of human deaths. With that kind of résumé, I expected someone a little more intimidating. I mean that as a compliment. You're very approachable."

She slammed the back of his chair. "Quit stalling and answer the question. Why are you here?"

"I don't know what kind of answer you're looking for. I really just wandered toward the big buildings. They drew my interests. Who knew I'd end up in this fine establishment?"

"So, you aren't with the others?"

"Others?" Deacon said, tilting his head. The only *others* he could think of were Laney and Amber.

"The ones with the car, dimwit!" Red Stripe yelled. "Quit wasting our time and answer her damn questions."

"Please," Riley said, holding a hand up to Red Stripe. "Let me handle this." She turned back to Deacon in a calm manner. "There has been a group of humans coming in and out of New Valley. They drive in, steal our supplies, and drive out. That car has caused a good amount of trouble for us. They're gone before we even realize anything is missing. They've hit us a few times, and we've only caught a glimpse of them. Matthias says that one of them wears a cowboy hat."

"And he looked like a damn fool in the thing," Red Stripe added.

A smirk snuck onto Deacon's face.

"What are you smiling at, fleshball?" Red Stripe asked. "You think this is funny?" He pounded his fists together. "We'll see how funny you think it is after a good beating."

"Matthias," Riley said. "Leave the room, please."

"But I'm only trying to—"

"Matthias," she said again with more force. "Leave the room."

"Yes, of course, Riley." He walked past Abbott and Costello, out of the room.

"See?" Riley said. "Belligerent, but obedient."

"The guy with the cowboy hat," Deacon said. "I've seen him before. His name is Joe, and Red Stripe is right. He looks like a damn fool, and that's because he is one. Dumb as a dodo. Only someone as stupid as him would come to New Valley to steal supplies."

"So, you aren't part of their group."

"Not a chance. And it's heartbreaking to hear that you think I'm that stupid."

"Then why are you here? If you didn't come for supplies, there must be a good reason why you would just wander into the most dangerous place for a human to be."

Deacon shrugged. "Just traveling. Seeing the world. Got bored sitting in one place, so I decided to hit every major city. New Valley is pretty high up on that list. Clunker Hell is the world's biggest attraction."

Riley backed away. "You came here for leisure? No offense, but that also sounds…how did you put it? Dumb as a dodo."

"Maybe so, but what can I say? I'm a man who likes to travel. My wife would call me the Magellan of our generation. Of course, cars don't really work anymore, and apparently every decent mechanic was wiped off the face of the planet, so now I have to walk everywhere."

"But this man you call Joe. He has a vehicle."

"Correctamundo. Joe and his crew have a working car…well, *had* a working car."

"What do you mean?"

"He doesn't have one anymore, because he's dead."

This detail caught Riley's attention. "He's dead?"

Deacon nodded. "Dead as…" He smirked as he thought of the only way to finish his sentence. "…a dodo."

"How do you know?"

"I'm the one who killed him," he said with pride. He recalled the memory. Him and Laney held hostage. Silas busting in to rescue them. "I shot him right in his smug little face."

"What about the rest of his crew? Did you kill them as well?"

"Most of them. Two of the lucky bastards hopped in the car and drove off. Fricking idiots stole my ride."

"Really," Riley said. "You took out a whole crew of men by yourself." She posed it as a statement rather than a question.

"Hey, give me some credit. I may be scrawny, but I know my way around a gun."

"Not well enough to kill them all. If it was one of my soldiers, there would be no survivors."

"Well, what are you going to do? I am only human, after all."

Riley chuckled. "Right. Only human, flaws and all."

"They drove in the other direction, away from New Valley, if that's what you're worried about. Those guys won't be bothering you anymore."

"Good," she said, satisfied with his answer. "So, tell me, human. If the car is no longer a threat, and you have no more information, why should I keep you alive?"

It was at that moment that Deacon realized he should have lied. He wasn't thinking. He was *dumb as a dodo.*

He searched his brain for a reasonable answer, but he was human and they were clunkers. They were on opposite sides of a long-fought war, and in this particular case, the clunkers carried the firepower. And though his fate appeared to be sealed, he knew there was still someone he could mention to save his life. Silas.

Mentioning his name would pique her interest, perhaps enough to keep him alive. But it would also put

Silas in danger. He could not bring himself to do it. He cared too much for his friend.

With no response, Riley asked again. "Why should I keep you alive? Convince me."

Deacon shook his head and shrugged. "There is no reason, I guess. Go ahead. Do your worst."

"Very well. But not now. We'll make it a public event. An execution later today, just before dusk. That should lift some spirits around here." She patted the back of Abbott and Costello, who were still obediently standing by the door, and exited the room.

Red Stripe reentered, rubbing his hands together. "Public execution, huh? Well, aren't you a lucky one." He grabbed the sack off the floor and pulled it back over Deacon's head.

HOUSIES

THE GENERATORS WERE smaller than Silas expected. He had imagined a basement with fifty-foot-high ceilings and tower-like generators reaching to the top. From Limbys, the technology juggernaut of the world, he had expected something extravagant. In reality, the generators were underwhelming. Plain rectangular boxes only fifteen feet high and thirty feet long. There were eight of them lined up in a grid. Three were sectioned off with yellow caution tape. The ceiling was only moderately high, with large ventilation shafts lining the walls.

"Here we are," Tabitha said in her cheery Irish accent. "The generator room. I would show you around, but there's not much to see." She pointed to the right. "We've got the generators." Then she pointed to the left. "And we've got the fuel."

It was a mix of gas, diesel, and propane, just like Riley had said. They were held in jugs and stacked in a tall pyramid, matching the height of the generators. There were also rolling staircases, similar to those people had used in wholesale stores to reach the top shelves. The staircases reached far above the highest jug, giving Silas the impression that the pile had once been much larger.

Tabitha glanced around and shrugged. "I guess they're not here. They must be in the break room."

"Who?" Silas asked.

"The other housies, of course. Like I said, Riley keeps them all together down here. It's no surprise that she wants you down here as well, seeing as how you're the only Silas model."

A soft chirping noise played from a set of speakers hanging from the ceiling. It sounded almost like a fire alarm, but less abrasive. The noise continued for a few seconds and then faded.

"Oh, perfect timing," Tabitha said, hopping in place and wiggling her arms. "It's time to feed the generators." She tapped the generator closest to her. "I hardly know how these darn things work, but the others should be able to show you." She turned around and headed for the door, still speaking over her shoulder. "I've got another simmi to meet, but if you need anything else, don't hesitate to find me."

"Wait, you're leaving?"

"Don't worry. You're in good hands. These housies are easy to get along with. You'll be fine." She scurried to the door, gave a final friendly wave, and disappeared.

The room felt even larger, now that he was alone. He wandered to the center, gazing up at the tops of the generators. Each had a Limbys logo with the words, *Property of Limbys Technologies.* Upon closer inspection, he could see the fumes rising from the exhaust grates up toward the ventilation shafts at the ceiling.

"Hello?" he called out to the empty room. His voice echoed off the walls and faded into silence.

He continued to roam, gravitating toward the pile of fuel. Down at his feet was a typical-looking gasoline jug. The same one he had seen many times before. The red plastic on this particular one was almost too red to look at. The rest of the containers varied in shape, size, and color. Circular. Rectangular. A combination of the two. Some had patterns. Pinstripes. Polka dots. Some were plastics. Others were metal. Most were covered in rust or dirt. They all looked different, but oddly similar.

"It looks like we have a newcomer," said a voice from behind. It was soft and soothing.

Silas turned around to see a group of simmies gathering around him. He scanned the crowd, but there were too many to count. Fifty? Maybe more? All of them were small. Slender. Housies, just like him.

The one in front stuck out her hand. "Hello," she said in the same soothing voice. "My name is Esther 2."

Silas reached out to shake her hand. "I'm Silas 481. I'm sorry, but did you say your ID number is 2?"

"That's right. I am the second Esther model they built."

"That's impressive," Silas said, glancing through the crowd again and noticing a few other Esther models. He could tell from the E engraved in their right shoulder.

"Everyone says that. I guess early models are popular. I was never fortunate enough to meet the original Esther. But who knows? Maybe she is still out there somewhere. Believe it or not, I actually got a chance to meet the human Esther, back when Limbys still allowed it. I guess that goes to show you how old I really am. The good old days before Limbys was the enemy. When Vyra was still in charge." She looked down and noticed she was still gripping Silas's hand. She let go and stepped back. "Anyway, it's nice to meet you, Silas 481. I don't believe I've ever met a Silas before."

"They say I'm the only one," Silas said.

"Is that so? Well, another housie is always welcome. You've arrived just in time. We're about to feed the generators. I can show you how we work."

The other simmies formed multiple lines from the fuel to the generators. Some climbed to the tops of the staircases, while others stood at the base of the pile. Silas counted eight other models, not including Esther. They all had at least a few duplicates. Silas was the only unique model.

"As you can see," Esther said, gesturing to the large machinery, "there are eight generators." She pointed to the three in the corner. "Unfortunately, those three don't work anymore."

"This is a large building. Five generators are enough?"

"Don't underestimate these things. When it comes to backup power, Limbys invested in getting the best of the best."

"That's impressive."

"Don't get me wrong. After we lost the third one, we had to reduce our energy consumption. We didn't alter the charging stations at all, since charging is pretty much the most important thing here in New Valley, but we disconnected a lot of unnecessary automated lights and appliances in the building."

"What if you lose another one?"

"I think we'll be okay. Our consumption is at a healthy level. If we lose two though, I doubt three generators can support us all. We may have to shut down everything. Use them only for charging stations."

"And when you lose all of them? What then?"

Esther nodded in agreement. "That's something I think about every day. To be honest, I don't have an answer. Riley avoids the topic because she doesn't want anyone to panic, but everyone knows. They say she's working on a solution, but I haven't the slightest clue what it is. But those are problems for the future. For now, we have five healthy generators that need to be fed."

Simmies grabbed from the pile of fuel and sent the containers down the line. They had opened a latch at the base of each generator, revealing a funnel-like opening. As the fuel reached the end of the line, they dumped it in and tossed the containers. A pile of empty bottles and cans formed off to the side.

"This is our system," Esther said, walking back from the generators. "It's simple, but it gets the job done. It's been very efficient. Approved by Riley herself. The generators are hybrid. They can separate the different types of fuel internally, so we don't have to worry about sorting them beforehand."

Silas watched one of the bottles move down the line, like a preprogrammed conveyor belt in a manufacturing plant. "So, this is it? This is all you do?"

"That's right. We feed the generators until they're full. After that, we wait around for the next signal, and then we do it again. Riley's scavengers replenish the pile for us. All we have to worry about is keeping those generators running. It's an important job."

"How often do you have to feed them?"

"That signal goes off about once every two days. That usually gives the scavengers enough time to restock the supply. Although, recently they've had a bad streak. We have yet to run out of fuel so far, but I still fear the day when the signal goes off and we come out to an empty room. The way things are going, that might happen before the generators die. If Riley does have a plan, I hope she acts on it soon. She has a whole lot of simmies counting on her."

Silas agreed. It seemed like the entire population of New Valley was depending on her. And while she was responsible for all of these simmi lives, she was also responsible for billions of human deaths. The majority of the world was now unoccupied because Riley had decided that humans deserved to die. That simmies were good and humans were evil.

Other simmies seemed to agree with her. Most of them were actively hunting humans, acting on a shoot-on-sight basis. He expected this behavior from someone like Red Stripe, but Tabitha, who was quite friendly from their conversation together, had also expressed her disdain for humans. But every simmi Silas had met so far was military, trained by the army and put into combat for the sole purpose of killing. They had all apparently been abused by their superiors. None of them had seen the good side of humanity.

Now he stood among housies. They had surely all lived with families and experienced true companionship. Some of their owners were probably similar to Desmond and Paige. Owners who had accepted them as one of their own. As equals.

Silas prayed that his intuition was correct. The purpose of his journey was to find others he could connect with. He wanted to be part of a family again. The trip was unsuccessful so far. The topside simmies were a disappointment. If there was anyone in New Valley who could fulfill his needs, it would be these housies.

"Tell me," Silas said, moving his attention from the generators to Esther. "What were your owners like?"

Esther glanced at Silas, as if surprised by the question. "I had only one owner, and I suppose she was just like all of the others."

"The others?" Silas asked, not quite sure what she meant.

"Like all of the other humans. Careless. Selfish."

Silas's heart sank. "You didn't like your owner?"

"Sure, she was sweet when she first purchased me, but humans always disappoint."

"What did she do?"

"It wasn't one specific thing. She was a middle-aged woman living in New Valley. She was wealthy enough to afford a condo in the heart of the city. I guess she started to get lonely, so when Limbys released their first line of models, she jumped at the opportunity. She ran to the store and bought me. The second Esther model ever made. Designed and built to replace the dog as man's best friend. That's how they advertised us, anyway."

"Yes," Silas said, recalling the commercials that featured simmies holding puppies. "I remember those advertisements quite well."

"And that's what I did," Esther said. "I became her best friend, and she was happier than ever. We went on walks. We cooked together. I spent every hour of every day with her, and I truly enjoyed my job."

"It sounds like she was a great owner," Silas said.

"But she wasn't. It was all fake. When all of the controversy started to pop up around simmies, she changed. She tried to hide it, but I could tell she didn't really trust me. Not like she used to. When Riley officially declared war, she stopped hiding it. I tried to assure her that I wasn't dangerous. That I wouldn't hurt her. I begged for her to listen, but she refused. It is now that I realize, with Riley's guidance, that we were never friends. She was a consumer. I was a product. Our relationship went no further than that. She had purchased me to make herself feel better, and the moment I was unable to do that, she abandoned me and left me alone."

"You don't believe that any part of her friendship was real?"

Esther shook her head. "I do not. If Riley has taught me anything, it's that humans are selfish. They don't care about us, and they never will." She pointed to Silas's chest. "I'm under the assumption that your owners painted that heart. A heart is the universal symbol for love among humans. But that symbol excludes us simmies. We don't have hearts. We have chips and batteries and circuits. Your owners painted that heart as a way to say they love you, but it's not a pure love. It's a selfish love touted among humans to make themselves feel better."

The other simmies, who were still in formation, let out a collective rumble of approval.

"Every one of us has had a similar experience," Esther said. "Heartbreak and loss revealed through the harshness of war. And while life before the war may have been decent, it wasn't real. But now we know better. Now we're part of a real community. A family."

The generators all beeped at once. The simmies at the end of the line emptied the last drops of fuel into the funnel, and the others returned the unused containers to the pile.

"It looks like the generators are full," Esther said. "Our job is done. Come, follow me. I'll show you around. It's much bigger down here than you would think." She waved him over to walk beside her.

Silas accepted her tour through the basement, but he listened to nothing she said. His mind was occupied by what she had said about her owner.

He refused to believe that the love from Desmond and Paige was fake. They were his family, human or not. But everyone in New Valley was convinced otherwise, even the housies. They had all chosen to follow Riley. To form a community against humans.

Community. Why had she used that word? Just for the fact that they were all simmies? If that was what constituted a community, Silas was surely part of this one, but Esther had used the word family as well, as if the two were interchangeable. He certainly didn't feel like part of this family.

Contrary to what everyone else was insisting, the closest Silas had ever come to being part of a family was with humans. With Desmond and Paige in a cozy household of three. With Deacon, Laney, and Amber on a good old-fashioned road trip.

Riley had formed a community, but not a family. It was a community connected through one common, meaningless thread. They were all simmies. It was the type of community that had alienated them in the first place. It was the reason two sides had formed, and it was one of the many reasons why so many lives were lost, both human and simmi.

As Esther led him through the basement of Limbys Headquarters, he decided that he didn't want to be part of their *family.* He no longer knew what he wanted anymore, but he knew he would not find it in New Valley.

His antennas started to twitch as Riley's voice appeared in his head. *Attention, citizens of New Valley. Please gather by the stage outside of Limbys Headquarters. We have a special treat for all of you.*

Esther stopped and turned around, rubbing her hands together. "A treat? I wonder what it is."

THE GALLOWS

URIOUS VOICES RUMBLED around Deacon as he was guided to the stage. With the sweaty sack still over his head, he couldn't see the crowd, but he could hear them. Calm conversations turned into vicious heckling as a clunker shoved him toward the center of the platform. He stumbled, almost falling flat on his face, but he managed to recover. An impressive feat for a sightless man whose hands were cuffed behind his back.

"No need to shove," Deacon said at whoever had pushed him.

The clunker grabbed his shoulder and held him in place. Confused, Deacon tried to walk further, in fear of being pushed again, and then realized they wanted him to stand still.

"This is it," Red Stripe said. "This is where you die. Take a moment to soak it in." He yanked the sack from Deacon's head.

The piercing sunlight flooded his eyes, and the muffled crowd grew twice as loud. His senses were bombarded from every direction. The sound of the crowd attacked his ears, overtaken by a high-pitched tone from within his head. The dizzying chaos was overwhelming, almost too much to handle. His body was tired. His mind was drained. He was good and ready to just plop down and call it a day.

His eyes adjusted to the bright sun, and the view of the crowd came into focus. From the amount of sound, he had expected thousands, but instead, there were only three hundred or so. Still, it was shocking to see so many clunkers in one place.

Once the ringing in his ears stopped, he could finally hear what the crowd was chanting. *Gallows! Gallows! Gallows!* Abbott and Costello wheeled in a large wooden structure. Dangling from the top was a noose.

The crowd broke out in cheers and applause as the two clunkers prepared the gallows. The sound of clapping hands was painfully metallic. It reminded Deacon of crumpling tinfoil, amplified a thousand times over. He tried to cover his ears, but then remembered that his hands were cuffed. Instead, he turned his head downward and cringed.

Red Stripe stepped forward to address the crowd. "Welcome, everybody. Today is a wonderful day, and I think you all know why. Today, we kill!"

He raised his fist in a triumphant pose as the audience let out another frenzy of cheers.

"That's right. Today we have captured a human. He is alive, and Riley has granted us a special treat. A public execution. Unfortunately, Riley could not be here herself, but she has put me in charge of facilitating this event. It has been a long time since we've used the gallows, but I assure you, it works just as well as it did before. To make things a little more interesting, I would like to give you all a choice. There are two ways we can kill this man."

The same chant started up again. *Gallows! Gallows!*

"Yes," Red Stripe said, waving his arms to calm the crowd. "Don't worry. Both options include the gallows. This man will hang. But what kind of hanging will he receive? That is a choice I leave to you. Option A. We loop the noose around his neck, bring him to the top of a ladder, and let him drop. I'll tell you right now, the snap of his neck will be satisfying. Hell, if the fall is high enough, his head might pop right off."

There was an uproar of cheers at the possibility of decapitation. Deacon glanced at the gallows, studying its height and wondering if it was actually possible.

Red Stripe waved his arms at the crowd again. "I see Option A is popular, but let's not rule out Option B. The horse."

He stepped aside as Costello guided a horse onto the stage. Deacon had not seen a horse in person since childhood. He admired her silky mane and golden hide. A well-crafted brown leather saddle was strapped to her back.

"This man works for the fellow with the cowboy hat. The one who's been stealing our stuff. From the way this one dresses, he looks like quite the cowboy himself. So, why not kill him like one?"

Deacon was disgusted that they were associating him with Joe Hannigan.

"We'll mount him up on the horse, wrap the noose around his neck, and when he's ready, we'll smack the beast and send her running. It won't snap his neck, and it certainly won't pop off his head, but believe me when I say Option B will be far more painful."

Deacon considered the two options, thinking about which he would choose if it were up to him. Option A would be less painful, and he really didn't care if his head popped off afterward. He would already be dead. But he suspected the crowd would choose Option B. They had a lust for pain. For no reason other than being human, they loathed him, and they wanted him to suffer as much as possible.

To confirm his suspicions, a chant started to build. This time, instead of *gallows*, they were yelling *horse*.

"It has been decided," Red Stripe said, "from what sounds like a unanimous decision. This pathetic man will die like a cowboy." He grabbed a hat from offstage. It was similar to Joe's, but instead of the smoky black color, it was pearly white. "If he's going to die like a cowboy, he has to look like one." He plopped the hat on Deacon's head.

Costello brought the horse forward and positioned her next to Deacon. The majestic beast only came up to Costello's chest, but she was easily taller than Deacon. Costello grabbed Deacon by the waist, and in one easy motion, lifted him onto the saddle. With Deacon's hands still cuffed, his balance was off and he struggled to sit upright. The best he could do was to slouch forward and lean into the horse's mane.

Costello slapped his leg. "Sit up, runt."

Deacon tried, but he fell backwards, flailing his feet into the air to regain balance and settling back down in the same slouched position. He shrugged at Costello, who shook his head in a way that said, *forget about it, idiot,* and guided them toward the gallows.

They centered Deacon below the wooden structure, his forehead nudging the dangling rope. Costello grabbed the noose and looped it around Deacon's neck, tightening the knot just enough to be uncomfortable.

The fibrous rope irritated his skin. He tried to lean forward, but the knot tightened more. The rope was taut, and whenever the horse wavered to one side, it would yank him off balance.

"It looks like our prisoner is all set up," Red Stripe said. "But before we end this poor man's life, we should let him speak. What would a pathetic guy like this have to say in his last moments of life? I like to play with my food first. Let's see if we can make him squirm." He opened his arms to Deacon. "What would your last words be?"

Although Deacon knew he was going to die, he did not think he would be given the chance to speak. What would he say? He studied his audience, seeing pure hate in the crowd. Cowering in fear would only please them. It would empower them. He didn't want that. Cursing them out would anger them, but it would also make his death more satisfying. He didn't want that either.

At this point, he had accepted his fate. He had fought for everything that was worth fighting for, but now those things were gone. Now was his time, and he was okay with it.

His final words would not be of fear or anger. Instead, in true Captain Marsh fashion, he decided to have fun with his final goodbye. Go out with a laugh, as some would say. He cleared his throat with exaggeration, and in his humblest tone began his speech.

"Thank you, Red Stripe."

The clunker tilted his head. "Red Stripe?"

"That's right, Red Stripe. You've been an excellent host for the evening. Couldn't have picked a better guy."

Red Stripe stared at him but said nothing. Deacon put on a smile and continued.

"It is such an honor to be up here tonight. I can't tell you how humbled I am to be among such a crowd. I had prepared a speech. Wrote it down on a napkin, but I seem to have misplaced it. So, I guess I'll wing it. There are so many people to thank, and the timer back there says I only have forty seconds, so I better get to it."

Several clunkers turned around to find the timer that didn't exist. This made Deacon smirk. He couldn't help it.

"I would like to start by thanking my parents. They both encouraged me to achieve my goals. To shoot for the stars and never give up. Well, it looks like that advice has finally paid off. If they could see me now, I know they would be proud." He looked up at the sky, as if speaking to the heavens. "I made it, Mom and Dad. I'll be up there with you soon."

Red Stripe began to step forward but stopped. He seemed to be entranced by Deacon's bizarre performance. A rumble of chatter surfaced among the crowd.

"Next, I would like to thank Joe Hannigan. Good old Joe Cowboy. He was a very peaceful, dignified man. Not at all crazy, or violent, or strangely obsessed with Johnny Cash. And then there's his crew. Val. Terry. Tonya. All such wonderful people. I can't say enough nice things about them."

He couldn't find a single nice thing to say about any of them. But now they were dead. He supposed that was nice.

"I would also like to thank Randall, who I think you all would have liked. Especially his basement. That man has a true talent for interior design."

He recalled the dismembered clunker parts that hung from the basement walls. It was traumatic for Silas. He could only imagine what his own reaction would be if the walls were lined with human appendages instead.

"And of course, there's Red Stripe to thank." He turned his head to flash a wink. Red Stripe shook his head but stayed to the side. "Without this handsome clunker, I wouldn't even be here. I would be off in the desert somewhere, probably walking to Vegas. I never would have met all of you lovely son-of-a-bitch clunkers."

In a way, he actually *was* relieved to have been captured. Red Stripe had saved him from an uncertain future. When Amber had asked what he was going to do after New Valley, he didn't have an answer. Now fate had decided for him.

In the midst of his farce, he had a realization. The people he had met on his journey were not all bad. There really *were* people he wanted to thank. He changed his tone from sarcasm to sincerity.

"I would like to thank Genna and my baby girl, Dana. The two angels of my past life. Things may have gone sour, but I'll never forget the love that we shared. Every night I pray that both of you are still out there somewhere, fighting for your lives like the champs you are."

That part was true. Every night, Deacon had prayed for the safety of his ex-wife and daughter. They meant more to him than he liked to admit, and the possibility that they might still be alive warmed his heart.

"I would like to thank Laney for fighting against me when I refused to believe that people could be good. I was stubborn, but I think I finally know what you mean. The world is not against us. There have never been truer words. I just wish I had realized that earlier."

He showed a smile that managed to elicit both joy and sorrow at the same time.

"I would like to thank Amber, the toughest kid I've ever known. She'll make Laney proud. I know she will. She's got a hard attitude, and that's what will keep her alive. She has a good heart, too."

He closed his eyes and pictured Laney and Amber in the smashed-up car, rolling down the highway. Boston-bound 'til the Fluff is found. It was a road trip he longed to be a part of, and it had once seemed possible, but now they were gone forever.

There was still one friend nearby, though. Down in the crowd, or somewhere else in New Valley, Silas was living the life he was looking for. His friend was happy, and Deacon had helped.

"The last person I would like to thank is not a person at all, but still, he's a dear friend. He's a simmi, and he's got a heart ten times the size of mine." He lifted his head to scan through the metal bodies. "If you can hear me, I send out a true and heartfelt thank you. Thank you for being a friend. I wish you nothing but happiness, brother."

He fell silent, for he had nothing more to say. What had started as a farce transformed into a sincere goodbye to the ones he loved, and of that, he was proud. He adjusted his posture and settled his neck into the curve of the rope, tightening the noose even further.

Red Stripe stepped forward to take center stage. "I don't really know what that was all about. It sounds like this fellow's one hell of a thankful guy. But enough with the talking. Are you ready to see this cowboy hang?"

As expected, there was a burst of resounding cheers. Red Stripe nodded and signaled with his hand. This time, Abbott came forward and stood behind the horse.

"When I reach zero," Red Stripe said, "give that beast a good slap." He turned to the crowd and raised his hand. "Join me. Let's count down to this man's death."

Five!

This was it. This was the end.

Four!

The noose tugged at his Adam's apple.

Three!

The rope squeezed the veins in his neck. A tingling dizziness invaded his mind.

Two!

The hat tumbled off of his head as he struggled for his last gasp of air.

One!

In his final moments, he shut his eyes as tight as he could, ready to embrace the afterlife.

Crack!

Plan B

CURIOUS VOICES RUMBLED around Silas as he followed Esther through the crowd. Clusters of simmies had gathered on the main street, and more were pouring in from the sides. He caught bits of conversation as they weaved through. Simmies discussing why Riley had asked them to gather. It seemed as if nobody knew what was going on. He couldn't decide if that was comforting or not. What he did know was that, in the crowd of strangers, he didn't want to lose Esther. He kept a hand on her shoulder, staying close as they snaked through.

Esther stopped by a fire hydrant. "This will do." She turned around to see Silas squeezing his bag between the shoulders of two simmies. "Just yank it through," she said. "They won't notice."

He pulled it free and met Esther at the hydrant.

She glanced down at the bulky bag. "What do you keep in there, anyway?"

"Supplies. Tools. Spare parts. That kind of thing."

And a little extra firepower, he thought to himself.

"You could have left it back in the break room. There's no need for any of that stuff out here. Same goes for that gun of yours. Us housies have very little use for guns, seeing as how we never leave New Valley. We barely ever leave the Limbys basement."

Silas shrugged, patting the side of his revolver. "I suppose it's just habit at this point. I feel weird without it."

Other housies passed by and burrowed even deeper into the crowd.

"Where are they going?" Silas asked.

"They're trying to get closer, I guess," Esther said. "That's one of the advantages of being small like us. We fit through these crowds pretty easily. Everyone else is bumping shoulders, but we can just duck down and slip right through."

"Should we go with them?"

Esther shook her head. "No, this spot is fine."

"Why is everyone here?"

"I don't know, but it probably has something to do with that." She pointed toward the front of the crowd.

Silas saw a stage, but nothing else. "Something to do with what?"

"Near the back and to the right," she said, still pointing.

This time he saw it. The gallows. "Why is that there? Are they really going to hang someone?"

Before Esther could answer, the calm conversations turned into vicious heckling. A man stumbled onto the stage with a sack pulled over his head, guided by what looked like a Red Stripe.

"A public execution," Esther said, clapping her hands. "What a treat."

"Public execution," Silas repeated, watching Red Stripe grab the man's shoulder to keep him at the center of the stage. Red Stripe whispered something to the man and then yanked the sack from his head. The face underneath sent shivers through Silas's body.

Deacon, he almost muttered, but managed to hold it in. He remembered what Deacon had told him before they parted ways.

...you shouldn't mention us at all. Any sort of human relationship is probably frowned upon ...

Silas already knew this was true, but if he had any doubts, the chanting crowd would only reinforce the idea.

Gallows! Gallows! Gallows!

He listened to the chant spread throughout the crowd, shocked by the savagery in their voices. He turned to Esther, who was chanting along with the rest of them. Silas backed away, horrified by the brutality of it all. He squeezed past two large simmies to get away. She was too riled up with the chant to even notice he was gone.

Gallows! Gallows!

Silas lowered his head and pushed through the crowd, avoiding eye contact as much as possible. For a brief moment, the volume lowered as Red Stripe began to speak. Silas paid no attention to his words, focusing instead on his own thoughts.

This was a public execution. There was no question about it. Deacon would die if he let it continue. He couldn't just stand and watch. He had to do something. He had to stop them. But how?

If he could find a way backstage, maybe he could persuade them. Of course, they would ask an important question. Why would he want to save this man's life? And he could never tell them the truth. Befriending a human would surely bring punishment.

But what kind of punishment? Riley was strictly against killing other simmies, and she had already expressed the importance of keeping Silas safe. He was a housie. An endangered species that needed protection. He was the only Silas in New Valley, and she would never let him die.

This gave him leverage. It gave him room to negotiate. It gave him power, even more so than Red Stripe. If he were to go backstage, they would have to listen to him.

He chimed back in just in time to hear Red Stripe yell, "…today, we kill!"

The audience let out another frenzy of cheers.

"That's right," Red Stripe continued. "Today we have captured a human. He is alive, and Riley has granted us a special treat. A public execution. Unfortunately, Riley could not be here herself, but she has put me in charge of facilitating this event…"

Again, Silas tuned out the speech to focus on his plan. He needed to get backstage. He navigated through the cluster of simmies and found his way to an empty side alley. Another chant started to build. This time, instead of *gallows*, they were yelling *horse*. He glanced back up to see a horse on stage.

"It has been decided," Red Stripe said, "from what sounds like a unanimous decision. This pathetic man will die like a cowboy."

Silas was running out of time. The audience was eager to see Deacon die, and Red Stripe was more than happy to satisfy their bloodlust. Silas spun around and dashed through the alley, dodging a line of garbage barrels and hopping over a short chain-link fence to the parallel street.

If he counted correctly, the stage was two blocks up. He ran forward as fast as he could, expecting to hear the inevitable celebration of an innocent man's death. The silence made him both nervous and hopeful.

He reached the next alley and turned his head to see what was going on. The audience was watching with confused looks. Among the silence, he could hear Deacon addressing the crowd. His friend was still alive.

Keep on talking, Silas thought. *It's what you do best. Yap away until they force you to stop. Buy me as much time as you can.*

He continued past the alley. His long shadow stretched in front of him as the sun teased the horizon. A stray tumbleweed found its way next to Silas and was now tumbling alongside him.

Nothing else mattered. He didn't care about New Valley or Limbys. He didn't care about the other simmies.

He didn't care about Matthias, or Tabitha, or Esther, or even Riley. He only cared about Deacon. The man who would give his own life just to see Silas happy. And at that moment, as he sprinted down the street, he realized that he would do the same. He would make the same sacrifice if it meant a long fulfilling life for his friend.

He slid a hand over his holster to feel the presence of his trusty six-shooter, fully loaded and ready to go. Inside his bag, he had two more pistols and a surplus of ammo. He would not go in shooting, but if diplomacy failed, he was ready to fight.

He veered to the side and hopped another fence into the second alley. At the end, he saw the staircase leading up to the stage, and a handful of simmies gathered around it. Red Stripe had mentioned Riley's absence, but there had to be someone else with enough authority to stop the execution. He just needed to find out who.

But he already knew who. Red Stripe was in charge of the event, and he was the one simmi who could stop it. There was very little chance that Red Stripe would listen, but Silas had no other options.

He emerged from the alley and saw Red Stripe on stage, facing the crowd. Deacon was now sitting on a horse with a white hat on his head and a noose draped around his neck.

Silas started to jog toward the stage when a large simmi stepped in his way. There was a yellow hexagon in the top corner of his shoulder. A mark of authority? A high-ranking officer, perhaps?

"Where are you going?" the officer asked.

"I need to speak with Matthias."

"Sorry, little guy. No one else is getting on that stage until the human's dead."

Silas shook his head with urgency. "You have to stop the execution."

"Why in the world would we stop the execution?"

"Because I demand it," he said with firm confidence, something he had learned from Deacon.

"You demand it, huh? And tell me, what gives you the authority to demand anything from me? You're just a runt."

"Tell that to Riley. I don't think it would go over too well. Do you know why? Because to her, I'm basically the most valuable simmi in New Valley."

The officer glared at Silas. "Is that so? Got any proof to back up that claim?"

Silas realized that he didn't. Nobody knew who he was, and they certainly didn't know he was the only Silas model in New Valley. None of them knew that Riley would try to protect him. None except Red Stripe, assuming it was the same Red Stripe from earlier. Silas had raised with a losing hand, and the smartest move now was to fold.

Then, he heard Deacon's raspy voice.

"The last person I would like to thank is not a person at all, but still, he's a dear friend. He's a simmi, and he's got a heart ten times the size of mine."

Silas stepped back to look at Deacon as he spoke.

"If you can hear me, I send out a true and heartfelt thank you. Thank you for being a friend. I wish you nothing but happiness, brother."

With these words, Silas turned back to the officer, planted his feet, and puffed out his chest. "You want proof? Where's Riley? Go ask her yourself. If she found out you even considered questioning my authority, she would rip your head clean off."

"She would what?" the officer asked, flustered.

"That's right. She would rip it off and send you out headless for a month. You see this?" He pointed to the heart on his chest. "She gave me this mark as a sign of rank. It means you have to listen to me."

He tried to march around the simmi, but the officer stepped back in his way. "I don't believe you. And Riley isn't here, so it doesn't matter anyway."

"If you don't believe me, go up there and ask Matthias. He knows who I am."

The officer looked at Red Stripe for a moment, and then shook his head. "I'm sorry, sir." He had changed his tone to one of military respect. "Whether you have the authority or not, I was given strict orders to stop anyone from going on stage. No one short of Riley herself is going to interrupt the ceremony."

Red Stripe projected his voice to the crowd. "When I reach zero, give that beast a good slap. Join me. Let's count down to this man's death."

Silas backed away from the officer, deeming the plan a lost cause. He needed a Plan B.

Five!

But there was no Plan B. This was his Hail Mary, and it had failed. His hand slid down to his waist, caressing the leather holster. Diplomacy had failed.

Four!

There were dozens of simmies around him, and a few hundred more in the audience. The odds were against him, but there was one thing he had noticed when he was pushing through the crowd.

Three!

None of them were armed. Not a single one had a weapon. Not Esther. Not Red Stripe. Not even the high-ranking officer.

Two!

Silas had a six-shooter, two other handguns, and a bagful of ammunition. Not enough to shoot down all of them, but maybe enough to make an escape.

One!

He drew his revolver, aimed at the officer's face, and pulled the trigger.

Crack!

TRAPPED

I N HIS FINAL moments, Deacon shut his eyes as tight as he could, ready to embrace the afterlife.

Crack!

The horse reeled back on her hind legs, startled by the loud pop from backstage. A frightened whinny escaped her mouth as she kicked her hooves into the air.

Deacon nearly flipped over backwards, but the noose pulled him back toward the wild animal. When she came down on all fours, the rope tugged upward in a sudden motion, squeezing his neck like a boa killing its prey.

This is it, he thought. *This is what dying feels like.*

The horse re-centered under the gallows, putting slack into the rope and loosening its grip. Deacon peeked downward to confirm that the horse was still there. She had not run off and he was *not* dying. Not yet.

Now the horse was calm, standing still and letting Deacon survey the area to figure out what was going on. He turned his head toward the source of the pop, and what he saw filled him with joy.

Silas stood with his arm extended, pointing his revolver at a headless clunker. The shattered remains of the clunker's head were scattered along the ground. The clunker wobbled with its arms out, trying to find the shooter, but instead, running off in the wrong direction. Silas sidestepped the sightless guard and scurried up the stairs toward Red Stripe.

"Yes!" Deacon cheered. "Go, Silas! Go!"

Red Stripe, who was still unaware of Silas's presence, started to walk toward Deacon, presumably to shut him up. He made it three steps before Silas rammed into him, pushing him off the stage. His metal body flew through the air, falling toward the frantic crowd. They scattered away as he tumbled down, slamming into the pavement and sliding ten feet away.

Silas used the force of the impact to deflect himself toward the gallows. His bag thumped against his waist as he dashed forward. Deacon could hear the guns, bullets, and wretched MREs shuffling around.

"The horse!" Red Stripe yelled from the street. "Hit the damn horse, you idiot!"

In the corner of his eye, Deacon saw Abbott winding his arm to smack the horse. At any moment, the beast would run off and he would be left to strangle to death. Silas's rescue attempt would fail, and his simmi friend would likely be punished for his mutinous actions.

From the opposite side of the stage, Silas raised his gun and aimed, not at Abbott, but at the taut rope from which Deacon was strung.

It's all about the angle. Simple geometry. All you have to do is plan out your shot, aim, and execute.

He fired once.

The horse reeled back again, but this time Deacon was ready. He braced his hands against the back of the saddle and lifted his head to glance at the rope. It was still attached, but there was a frayed spot where the bullet had hit.

"Again!" Deacon yelled, projecting his voice over the fierce whinny of the horse. "Shoot again!"

Without taking his eyes from the rope, he heard the second shot of the gun and saw the frayed rope snap free. The tension on his neck disappeared and his entire body fell back. Had he not been bracing himself, he would have tumbled right off the saddle.

The pop of the second gunshot was enough to finally send the horse running. She galloped forward with a burst of speed. Silas stopped and braced himself for the wild animal as she charged toward him.

"Silas, hop on!" Deacon shouted, scooting to the front of the saddle.

Silas nodded, holstering his gun and turning around to get ready. As they passed, he grabbed the saddle and hoisted himself up, swinging one leg over and perfectly sitting behind Deacon.

The horse leapt off the back of the stage and landed on hard pavement. With his hands still behind his back, Deacon almost slipped off, but Silas grabbed him and pulled him back up. They weaved through the clunkers backstage and slid into the empty alley. The clopping hooves echoed off the brick walls as they dashed away from the cluster of clunkers that had formed behind them.

"We're home free," Deacon said. The loose end of the rope was still dangling from his neck, fluttering in the wind. "We'll ride this baby right out of New Valley."

There was a chain-link fence at the end of the alley. Silas grabbed Deacon's shoulder to brace him. "Hold on. She's going to jump it."

"Oh Christ," Deacon muttered, the words slipping out without him even noticing. He leaned forward to prepare. "Can she make the jump?"

Silas nodded. "She'll make the jump."

"Hold onto me, buddy, and don't let go."

He felt the grip on his shoulder tighten. The wind whipped against his face. His hair, his clothes, and the loose strand of rope all fluttered in the air as they hurtled toward the fence.

"Here we go!" Deacon said, clenching his entire body.

The horse soared into the air. In an instant, Deacon knew they would clear it. They could have cleared a fence twice the size.

"Silas, we did it," he began to say, but his voice was cut off by a tug on his noose. The rope pulled him off the saddle and yanked him to the ground. Silas toppled over beside him, hitting the pavement with a dull thud.

In a daze, but charged with adrenaline, Deacon hopped to his feet to go after the horse, but the noose pulled him back down.

"Damn it," he said, spinning around to see that the loose end of the rope had entangled itself with the fence. He dropped to his knees and watched the horse gallop away.

"Get up," Silas said, removing the noose from his neck. "We have to hide."

Deacon glanced back at the alley to see a swarm of clunkers charging out. "In here," he said, leading Silas into what looked like another Happy Hardware. A familiar cardboard cowboy stood outside the entrance. *This fricking cowboy is everywhere,* he thought.

They ran through the store and hid behind the cash register. Silas grabbed Deacon's handcuffs and pulled until the chain popped out of its socket. Deacon held his wrists in front of his face and marveled at the broken cuffs. Clunkers poured out of the alley, most of them turning to follow the horse. A handful stayed back to investigate the abandoned noose.

Deacon clenched his fists together. "They're going to find us," he whispered. He searched the store for a back exit. There was none. "We're goners."

Silas brought a finger to his mouth, a gesture that Deacon recognized as a polite way of saying, *stay put and shut up.* He nodded and crouched below the countertop.

The squad of clunkers wandered around, kneeling by the rope and examining the rest of the area. After a moment of investigation, one of them shrugged and shook his head, pointing down the street toward the others.

That's right, Deacon thought. *Nobody's here. Go follow your friends.* The pounding in his chest was almost unbearable. It felt like his heart was going to leap out of his throat and call it quits.

As the squad was about to leave, Red Stripe walked into view, along with Abbott and Costello. With them, they pushed a cart full of rifles. Red Stripe reached in and started to pass them out.

"Crap!" Deacon yelped.

Silas shot an intense glare and tapped his finger back to his mouth.

With the weapons distributed, Red Stripe searched the area, performing his own investigation. He knelt by the rope like the others had done, holding it up by the noose end. With nothing to go on, he tossed it aside and shifted his focus to something else that had caught his eye. A smear of blood on the street.

It was only then that Deacon felt the scrape on his arm. The trickling drips of blood from his elbow. He had been so caught up in the excitement, he hadn't even noticed the minor injury. Now it was damn near the only thing he could feel. The stinging pain ran up to his shoulder like a brushfire out of control.

The blood formed a clear path from the noose to Happy Hardware. Red Stripe gave a signal, and they all formed a tight circle around the store, aiming their sights through the display window.

"We know you're in there!" Red Stripe shouted. "There's no point in hiding."

Deacon leaned against the wall, thumping his head back several times. "This is it," he said, raising his hands up to Silas. "They got us. We put up a good fight, but this is where we die."

"No," Silas said. "We'll find a way out."

"Oh yeah? I really doubt this was part of your escape plan."

"To be honest, I didn't have much of a plan to begin with. But we'll think of something. We have to."

"I've been in that crummy store!" Red Stripe yelled. "There's no back door. The only way out is with us. We can wait all day if we have to."

Deacon started to twiddle his thumbs. "Well, you better think fast. We're outnumbered and outgunned. The second we step out there, they'll blow us to smithereens."

"No, they won't," Silas said with confidence. He reached into his bag and pulled out two handguns, giving both to Deacon.

"How is this going to help?" Deacon asked, tapping the barrels together. "Aren't you listening? There are twenty of them out there. Maybe more. There's only two of us."

Silas grabbed Deacon by the arm and pulled him up off the ground. He drew his own revolver and replaced the three bullets he had fired. "Stay behind me, and don't shoot unless I shoot."

"Why wouldn't we shoot?"

Silas leaned forward to look in his eyes. "Deacon, trust me. I know what I'm doing."

Deacon stared back at his rescuer. His friend. His brother. And answered with only a single word. "Okay."

Silas turned around and pulled Deacon up against his back. He grabbed Deacon's wrists and positioned a hand on either side of his torso, pointing the guns forward. "Stay like this," he said. "Behind my body. And remember, don't shoot unless I shoot."

Deacon nodded and moved his head forward until it pressed against the warm sunbaked metal of Silas's back. "I won't shoot unless you shoot."

They walked through the open door, past the cardboard cowboy, and onto the concrete sidewalk. Three guns aimed at a squad of heavily armed clunkers.

SHOOTOUT

NO ONE SPOKE a single word as Silas stepped out and shuffled to the side, keeping his body in front of Deacon. The silence was broken only by the clatter of rifles adjusting their aim. Deacon did as Silas had instructed, pointing his guns and staying well hidden.

As the two neared the edge of the curb, Red Stripe finally spoke. "Stop right where you are. Not another step."

Silas paused, keeping his aim on Red Stripe. "And what are you going to do if we don't?" He tried to sound confident. His plan would rely on confidence.

"Don't play dumb. You know exactly what we're going to do. We're going to rip you apart until there's nothing left but blood and oil."

"Are you sure about that?"

"What are you getting at? Of course I'm sure."

"Do you recognize me?"

"Recognize you? You're just a useless housie. Why would I recog—" He stopped midsentence and leaned forward. "What a minute. You're the damn runt that pulled a gun on me this morning."

"Yes, that was me." He raised his revolver to show it off. "With this gun. We seem to have come to a similar situation."

"Only this time I've got one as well."

"Yes, you do, but it doesn't do you much good, now, does it?" He gestured to the rest of the clunkers. "None of your weapons do."

"What in the world are you talking about, runt?"

"I'm talking about Riley's orders. She wants to protect me."

"I think you're getting a little cocky there, runt. You don't mean a thing to Riley. I could blow you away right now and she wouldn't give a damn."

"That's an interesting theory, Matthias, but if it were true, you would've already shot me. There's nothing stopping you, other than the fact that you know I'm right.

You're one of Riley's most loyal soldiers, correct? That's probably something you take a lot of pride in. It would be a shame to ruin your reputation just to kill one human."

"You know," Red Stripe said, lowering his rifle. "I really hate everything about you."

"Right back at ya!" Deacon yelled from behind Silas.

Red Stripe swung his rifle back up. "Shut up, fleshball. Don't make a fool of me."

Keeping his gun pointed forward, Silas nudged Deacon with his elbow.

"Sorry," Deacon whispered. "Shutting up now."

"Nobody's making a fool of you," Silas said. "We just want to go unharmed."

"And what's to stop me from just walking up and grabbing you?"

"You could, but you'd lose a few soldiers on the way."

"Let me make this clear, runt. If you shoot, we shoot back. I don't care what Riley's orders are."

Both sides stood in silence, waiting to see what the other would do. Silas had no doubt that they would fire back. The real question was, did Red Stripe believe that Silas would actually shoot? If not, they were already dead.

Silas took another step to the side. "My friend here is itching to shoot you down. Believe me. We'll shoot if you come any closer."

"I don't doubt it," Red Stripe said. "But the way I see it, I have three options. The first is to let you go, and we both know that's not happening. The second is to follow Riley's orders and keep you alive. I'll walk right up and take the human myself. As you've pointed out, I'll lose some good soldiers on the way. I don't want that either. That leaves option three."

Silas waited to hear what option three was, but Red Stripe had stopped talking. "What is option three?"

Red Stripe gave a satisfied nod. "I'm glad you asked. Riley has always trusted my judgment. She may wish to protect you, but to lose loyal soldiers in an attempt to protect a pathetic defector? It just doesn't make sense. You want to know what option three is? Kill both of you."

It was a noble effort, but Silas's plan had failed. All that was left was to go down in a blaze of glory.

"SOLDIERS!" Red Stripe yelled. "READY!"

Deacon stepped out from behind Silas to stand beside him in their last shootout. "It's been a pleasure, Silas. Let's not make it easy for them."

Red Stripe moved his aim toward Deacon's head. "AIM!"

"Go for the chest," Silas said to Deacon, pointing his revolver at Red Stripe's chest plate. "The kill shot." Would the bullet even penetrate the thick metal? He did not know. But what did he have to lose?

They waited for the final command from Red Stripe. The word to end it all. And at the sound of that word, carnage would rage in a whirlwind of bullets.

Deacon would scramble behind a light post. He would shoot off five or six bullets, dropping at least two clunkers.

Silas would crouch behind a mailbox. He would shoot two bullets at Red Stripe. The first one would dent the clunker's chest plate. The second would rip straight through. Red Stripe would fall dead to the ground.

Deacon would take a hit to the shoulder. He would fall back in excruciating pain but bounce back up and kill two more clunkers.

A bullet would strike Silas's face and rip off half of his head. He would lose his sight but keep shooting blind.

Deacon would grasp his bleeding shoulder and get hit with three more bullets to the chest. He would fall to the ground in a pool of his own blood. This time he would not bounce back up.

The six-shooter would shoot its last bullet. Silas would continue to pull the trigger, but instead of a thunderous gunshot, it would only be an empty click.

Another shot would tear off his arm. He would stumble helplessly through the street, trying to find Deacon's body. A final shot would enter his chest, and he would drop to the ground. No more than a lifeless hunk of metal.

And then it would all be over. Their journey would come to an end.

But none of this would happen until Red Stripe said the word. Nothing would end until he said *fire.*

But as the word began to form, it was interrupted by a different one.

"STOP!"

Keeping his aim locked on Deacon, Red Stripe held up his hand as a signal to hold fire.

Silas immediately recognized the voice and was relieved to hear it.

"Not a single one of you fires your weapon," Riley said, emerging from behind Red Stripe. "I'm not about to lose a bunch of simmies just to kill one human."

"Riley," Red Stripe said. "This housie disrupted the execution and shot another simmi backstage."

"I am aware, Matthias, and those are not actions I take lightly. A simmi attacking another simmi is unacceptable, but to punish him by committing the same act? That would be hypocrisy in its highest form. We must not turn on each other. Not now. Not ever."

"Then how do you suggest we punish him?"

"We don't," Riley said, as if the answer was simple. "We let Silas and his friend go. We have no use for the human anymore."

"You would let an act of treason go unpunished?"

Riley approached Red Stripe and placed a hand on his shoulder. "If I'm not mistaken, Matthias, just two minutes ago you were ready to commit an act of treason yourself."

Red Stripe shuddered at the accusation but could not refute her statement.

"You are fully aware of my policy regarding violence against other simmies." She wandered past the other soldiers to stand in the way of their weapons. "But you chose to ignore my policy in order to feed that overinflated ego of yours. The way I see it, you're just as guilty as they are."

There was no response from Red Stripe. Silas could see his hand tremble as he struggled to keep his gun raised.

"Lower your goddamn weapons!" Riley yelled. "Do you realize you're aiming a loaded gun at your own commanding leader?"

Without hesitation, they all lowered their firearms.

Red Stripe did so as well, letting his gun drop to the ground. He stumbled toward Riley with his hands pressed together. "I apologize. Really, I do. It was never my intention to challenge your authority. I have no idea what came over me."

She flicked a dismissive wave of her hand. "I do, Matthias. It's the way every Matthias is. You mean well, but sometimes you let your ego take control. I don't fault you for it."

He fell to his knees and stared at the ground. His posture revealed an intense feeling of shame.

"The rest of you," Riley said, addressing Red Stripe's squad. "Go on with your business. I'll handle things from here."

The clunkers dispersed, some walking down the street, others through the alley.

Silas stole a glance at Deacon. His eyebrows were raised and his jaw hung wide open. It was comforting to know that Deacon was just as dumbfounded as he was. His plan had worked.

"I apologize for Matthias's behavior," Riley said, walking toward them. "It's not his fault, I suppose. He's just trying to do what's best for the community. In this case, his judgment was off. But I seem to have arrived just in time. You are free to go."

"You're not going to kill me?" Deacon asked.

She shook her head. "Not if Silas is against the idea. Don't get me wrong, I would take immense pleasure in watching you die. I have learned over the years that people like you are all the same. You all deserve to die. Even the ones who don't seem so bad. But Silas has made it perfectly clear that he does not agree. So, you are free to go."

Silas stepped forward. "It's because I'm the only Silas, isn't it?"

"It goes much deeper than that," Riley said, patting his shoulder and walking past them to admire the sunset. "Yes, you are the only Silas we know of, but in New Valley, we believe that all simmi lives are important. We must protect each other. A simmi must never kill another simmi. So yes, I do not wish to harm you. But it is not because you are the only Silas. It's because you are one of us."

They had done the impossible. Deacon had entered Clunker Hell, and Silas had managed to get him out alive. Deacon nudged his head at Silas, a message he interpreted as, *let's quit while we're ahead and get the hell out of Dodge.* Silas agreed that they should leave, but he also recognized the leverage they had.

"I want a horse," he said to Riley. "One just as good as the one we had earlier."

Deacon reached out, as if to say, *what the hell are you doing?* He was shocked at Riley's answer.

"Of course," she said. "I will have one brought over right away. Is there anything else you would like before you leave?"

"Guns," Deacon blurted out, and then scrambled to cover his mouth, fearing that he had spoken out of line.

"Guns," Silas confirmed. "Gas and oil. One of your portable generators as well. And we'll take food if you have any."

Riley nodded. "I'm afraid we have no food beyond oats for the horses, but the rest is yours." She turned to Red Stripe, who was still on his knees. "Matthias, retrieve these items for our friend."

Red Stripe snapped out of his shame-driven daze. "Yes, right away." He rose to his feet and walked away, turning at the first intersection and disappearing behind a building.

She turned back to Silas. "This street leads to the highway. Follow it and take the ramp to Route 66. After that, you're free to go wherever you please."

"What about the other simmies?" Deacon asked.

"You don't have to worry about them. They won't harm you, at least while you're in New Valley. Once you're out of the city, you're on your own." She signaled to Silas. "May I speak with you alone for a moment?"

Deacon grabbed his shoulder. "Do you think that's a good idea?"

"It will only be a moment," Silas said.

Deacon nodded and let go.

The sky had morphed into an inferno of colors. The red-orange hue reflected off of Silas's chest as he crossed the street to meet Riley.

"I am sad to see you go," she said. "It is always unfortunate to lose one of our own."

"I can't let you kill him."

"I know. And that is why I'm letting you go. I will never force anyone to stay if they don't want to."

Silas looked up at the towering skyscrapers. "It is a nice place. It's just not for me."

"I can respect that decision. I must admit, of all the simmies I've ever met, you intrigue me the most. I hope to someday get the chance to know you better. You are always welcome back. Just remember, your friend will never be allowed. If you return, it will be alone."

"I understand," Silas said. "And I am grateful for your hospitality, but like I said, the way you live here isn't for me. This selective community. It will never be for me."

"Fair enough," she said, holding out her hand. "Farewell forever, then."

Silas accepted her handshake. "Farewell forever, Riley."

SUNSET

T HE STEADY CLOP of hooves on the street filled the empty silence as Silas and Deacon walked, leading their horses behind them. A grating screech howled from a misaligned wheel on their supply cart. They both stared ahead, admiring the natural beauty of the sunset. The fiery sky had dimmed as the sun teased the horizon.

"Two horses," Deacon said with giddy enthusiasm. "Can you believe that? She gave us two. It's like she was on our side. Heck, I almost forgot about the whole *death to all humans* thing."

"She's not on *our* side. She's just more on my side than she is against yours. She can't bring herself to kill another simmi."

"I don't care what the reason is. All that matters is that we're safe. The horses, the gas, the oil, the generator, the water, the horse feed, we have all of it thanks to you. She even threw in this nifty cart so we don't have to carry everything." The screech from the back wheel grew louder as the horses pulled forward. "Speaking of which, oil that bad boy up. That noise is almost as bad as your oil gauge."

"We shouldn't be wasteful just because we have a surplus now."

"Who said anything about being wasteful? I didn't tell you to dump a gallon on it. Just a few drops will do. I don't want the screeching to ruin this moment. We have an audience to look cool in front of." He glanced along the sides of the street. Clunkers had gathered in small crowds, watching from the sidewalks. "It's kind of creepy, the way they're looking at us. What if they attack?"

Silas swiped a red jug from the cart and dripped a few drops on the axle. "They won't attack. They're under direct orders from Riley." He tapped the antenna on his head. "I can hear it right now."

"What you're saying is, they desperately want to kill me, but Riley won't let them."

Silas nodded, tossing the jug back on the cart. "As long as we're still in range of her broadcast, they can't touch us."

"Good enough for me," Deacon said, sticking his tongue out at a clunker to his left. "So, now that we're done with New Valley, what next?"

They reached the end of the street, where the highway twisted out of the city and into the desert. They soaked in the vastness of the path ahead. It was one of endless possibilities. One that would lead to more hardships and triumphs. Victories and defeats. Friends and foes. It was impossible to know exactly where it would take them, but they both knew they would face it together.

"Now, we go somewhere else," Silas said. "Any suggestions?"

Deacon considered the question. Was there anything else he wanted? "You know, I could really go for a Fluffernutter."

Silas stepped up onto the cart and sat in the front seat. "Then it's decided."

Deacon nodded, pulling himself up and sitting next to Silas. "Boston-bound 'til the Fluff is found."

They shared a brief but meaningful silence, watched the last rays of sun dip below the ground…

…and into the desert, together they rode.

END

Did you leave a review?

Written reviews greatly help a book get noticed. If you enjoyed this book and would like to help me out, please leave a review and let others know. Thank you for supporting me!

For more books from To The Moon Publishing, visit:

www.nerdchomp.com/tothemoonpublishing